Also by The Urban Griot

COLLEGE BOY

THE UNDERGROUND

ONE CRAZY A** NIGHT

Also by Omar Tyree

DIARY OF A GROUPIE

LESLIE

JUST SAY NO!

FOR THE LOVE OF MONEY

SWEET ST. LOUIS

SINGLE MOM

A DO RIGHT MAN

FLYY GIRL

cold blooded
A HARDCORE NOVEL

THE URBAN GRIOT

SIMON & SCHUSTER PAPERBACKS
NEW YORK   LONDON   TORONTO   SYDNEY

SIMON & SCHUSTER PAPERBACKS
Rockefeller Center
1230 Avenue of the Americas
New York, NY 10020

This book is a work of fiction. Names, characters, places, and incidents either are products of the author's imagination or are used fictitiously. Any resemblance to actual events or locales or persons, living or dead, is entirely coincidental.

Copyright © 2004 by Omar Tyree
All rights reserved, including the right of reproduction in whole or in part in any form.

First Simon & Schuster paperback edition 2004
SIMON & SCHUSTER PAPERBACKS and colophon are registered trademarks of Simon & Schuster, Inc.

For information about special discounts for bulk purchases, please contact Simon & Schuster Special Sales: 1-800-456-6798 or business@simonandschuster.com.

Designed by Karolina Harris

Manufactured in the United States of America

10 9 8 7 6 5 4 3 2 1

Library of Congress Cataloging-in-Publication Data
Tyree, Omar.
Cold blooded : a hardcore novel / the Urban Griot.— 1st Simon & Schuster pbk. ed.
p. cm.
1. African American criminals—Fiction. 2. Man-woman relationships—Fiction. 3. Saint Louis (Mo.)—Fiction. 4. Murder for hire—Fiction. 5. Chicago (Ill.)—Fiction. 6. Murderers—Fiction. I. Title.
PS3570.Y59C64 2004
813'.54—dc22   2004045444
ISBN 0-7432-6190-9

Dedicated
to the hustlers
the pimps
the players
the killers
and all of the women
who become addicted to them.

cold blooded

*M*oe . . . *Molasses* . . . *was the sexiest man I have ever been with in my life* . . .

It's strange sometimes to imagine what an adventurous young chick will do for the attention and company of an unpredictable man. Nowadays, or at least in black urban America, it seems that the most desirable cats, the real heartthrobs, are the coldhearted, thug niggas. Of course, most of them don't start off that way. They generally start off as rough around the edges mystery men, possessing obvious amounts of sex appeal that these young women find to be intoxicating. Such was the case with Janeia Goode and her man, Molasses, who were held up in a low-budget hotel room in St. Louis.

The digital clock on the oak-wood nightstand read 8:16 PM. Janeia stood not far from it, posing with her legs together in a black dress, with a high split up the right thigh. She was a caramel-coated diamond chick, sharper than a motherfucker. In the palms of her delicate hands she held the nickel-plated steel of a nine-millimeter pistol. She aimed it at the dresser mirror like a gangster chick.

"Spread your legs and lock your arms," Molasses's confident voice instructed her from behind. He stepped up and gripped her arms, while slowly kicking her feet apart against the deep gray carpeted floor. He wore a camel-colored wool suit with an off-white silk button-up shirt and no tie.

Janeia smiled at his touch, but only for a second before she pulled the trigger of the gun into her reflection in the mirror.

Click!

That's when Molasses smiled. He could feel the excitement running through her sexy-ass body as she continued to hold the unloaded pistol in her hands. She wanted his danger. He knew it from the moment she took his cell phone number when he first met her. She was patiently waiting at the bus stop on 83rd Street in their hometown of Chicago. She probably would have allowed him to drive her to her destination that day . . . if he had offered to.

He asked into her right ear as she handled his gun, "It feels powerful, doesn't it?"

Janeia looked into the mirror at his sly smile as he held her close from behind. He was dark and insatiable, like ghetto romance, determined to happen. A single platinum chain shone across his neck under his open-collar shirt. His hard-edged body was as firm as the steel of his gun.

In her response, Janeia nodded and grinned at him through her reflection in the mirror.

"Yeah," she answered. "I like power."

Molasses grinned and read the anticipation on her face. He then slid his hands away from her arms to caress her pert breasts. That was what she wanted, to be fondled the right way and undressed for seduction by a man who knew what the hell he was doing. Janeia had no patience for half-scared amateur niggas who would hesitate. A real man knew what he wanted and seized it with authority.

So Molasses kissed her back and unhooked her bra, like a real man would. He then nudged her head slightly forward with his, so that he could bury his lips into her hair, deep enough to find a naked spot on her neck to kiss.

And oh, how she melted when he reached down between

her legs and touched her there, while pulling down the spaghetti straps of her dress.

It was what she wanted, a real good fucking from a mysterious thug nigga. And when he undressed her and stretched her naked body across the bed to penetrate, Molasses even let her hold his gun against his bare back, while he spanked her where it felt good and made her squeal for Jesus to forgive her for her sins.

*. . . **but** I had no idea what he was really into.*

By the time the sweet heat of passion had cooled, the clock on the oak-wood nightstand read 11:05 PM. Janeia was still in bed, soaking up needed recuperation time, but Molasses was already fully dressed in a sharp, dark suit. He was calmly watching the clock.

He patted Janeia's shoulder in bed.

"You can finish sleeping in the car," he told her.

Molasses was the boss, and he had business back in Chicago in the morning. So Janeia took a last deep breath before climbing out of bed. She then entered the bathroom with her bag of necessities to freshen up and re-dress.

While she was still inside, Molasses loaded his gun and decided to speed up her pace a bit.

He spoke to her through the partially opened bathroom door.

"Look, ah, I hate to rush you, but I'm gonna run some of our stuff down to the car. Do you have everything you need in there?"

He waited for her response.

"Yeah, I have everything."

She was busy fixing her hair and clothes in the bathroom mirror.

Molasses nodded and was pleased with her response.

"Good," he told her. He grabbed the hotel key and two handfuls of their things. He slid his nickel-plated gun snugly into his bag of clothes.

Janeia smiled and shook her head, tickled by his candor. Molasses carried himself with an urgency that piqued her interest. So she quickened her pace to abide his pressing needs.

OUTSIDE, in the parking lot of their St. Louis hotel, a young white man sat in a black Lincoln rental car with Illinois license plates. He was dark-haired, slim, and studious, wearing a dark blue, zip-up jacket.

He watched in his rearview mirror as a sexy young white woman walked out from the hotel to reach her car, a black Mercedes SL.

She climbed inside, flipped down her vanity mirror, and checked her pretty face and dirty blond hair. She then started her ignition and drove off.

The young white man smiled with a thought in mind. The right amount of money bought even the homeliest guys the company of the finest women.

He then watched Molasses walk out from the same hotel, hands and arms loaded with luggage. After seeing Molasses, he immediately grabbed his cell phone and made a call.

Molasses opened the door of a dark GMC sedan and answered the ringing cell phone that had been locked inside the glove compartment.

"Is 'The Whale' alive at sea?" he asked into the receiver.

Charlie, the young white man, answered on the other line. He was sitting just a few cars away.

"Yeah, and he's all alone now."

Molasses kept his cool and nodded.

"I'll tell you about the boat ride in the morning."

"Just make it a *smooth* ride," Charlie advised him.

Molasses smiled and grunted, "Hmmph. Don't I always?"

"Ah, not exactly," Charlie told him.

Molasses grinned and hung up the cell phone. He slid it back into the glove compartment and reached into the backseat of the dark sedan. He pulled out a black leather carrying bag and climbed out of the car with it.

Molasses loaded the trunk of the car with the luggage and headed back toward the hotel. He still held the black leather carrying bag in his left hand.

Charlie drove off in the Lincoln.

BACK up in the hotel room, Janeia was finally ready to go. She was looking damned good, too, all curved out in the right places.

Molasses walked into the room, checked her out, and immediately smiled at her.

"Damn. I just had me a piece of that. I must be a lucky man."

Janeia grinned at him sheepishly. She looked down at his black leather carrying bag and casually asked him, "What's in the bag?"

Molasses blew her question off with an easy smile.

"Guys need carrying bags, too, sometimes. But hey, before we go, I found out that a friend of mine is staying in this same hotel. I want to walk down and pay him a surprise visit."

Janeia got excited. She was overjoyed to be a part of his world. What kind of friends did he have?

"Okay, sure. I'm looking good enough for a surprise, right?"

Molasses grinned at her and nodded.

"Yeah," he mumbled.

Janeia walked out with him. Molasses switched hands to hold the bag in his right and Janeia's in his left.

When they walked into the hallway toward the elevators, Molasses told her, "Let's just take the stairs. It's faster."

That was no big deal. So Janeia walked through the red-lit exit door and took the stairs with him.

They walked down two flights of stairs and entered the hallway on the sixth floor.

Molasses led her to room 612 and stopped. But instead of them knocking on the door for his friend, Molasses let go of Janeia's hand and pulled out a key card.

Janeia looked at him puzzled.

"What is that? You have a key to his room?"

Molasses looked at her sternly.

"Sometimes you don't need to ask so many questions. You just go with the flow," he told her.

Janeia didn't know what kind of flow he was referring to, so she was now on her guard. There wasn't any pass-the-panties train ride going on with her. So she prepared herself to let a motherfucker have it if they even tried her.

Molasses quickly opened the door to room 612 and walked in with Janeia beside him, standing apprehensively. He closed the door and locked it behind them. That made her even more apprehensive.

As they walked deeper into the room, an overweight white man jumped from his lounge chair to meet them. He wore only boxer briefs and a wife-beater tank top. His bed was still unmade from use.

"Who the hell are you? And how the hell did you get in here?" the man called "The Whale" snapped at the couple.

Molasses responded to him civilly.

"You don't remember me, Bob? I used to work for you out in Seattle."

The Whale began to back up toward his bed.

"My name is not fucking Bob. And you never worked for me."

Molasses began to smile.

"Aw, come on now, Harry. Don't tell me all black men look alike to you. We worked out in Seattle together. Remember?"

Janeia was confused. What the hell was going on? She didn't know what to make of things. She chuckled and shook her head, believing it was all some kind of a joke.

She even tugged at Molasses's hand to try and guide him back to the door. The joke had gone far enough, and she was not that amused by it.

The Whale grew irate and dipped low beside his bed as if he had a weapon there.

"I don't know who the hell you think you are, but I'll settle this right now!"

Molasses pulled out a long black gun from his black leather carrying bag. It had a silencer attached to the barrel. He held it in his right hand, while still holding Janeia's hand in his left.

"Slow your roll, John. Slow your roll," he told the man.

The Whale stopped reaching behind his bed and stood up straight and tall.

Molasses aimed the silencer gun right at the man's wide eyes. The Whale raised his hands with opened palms to surrender with poise. He figured he would try and talk his way out of it.

But Janeia began to panic.

"Shit! What the hell are you doing?"

She struggled in Molasses's grasp, but he continued to hold her hand tightly.

The Whale began to plead with him.

"Okay, who paid ya? I have money on me. I'll pay you more. We don't have to . . ."

Molasses fired his first shot into the man's neck to stop him from yapping.

Theessrrpp!

The Whale immediately grabbed at his throat as fresh blood squirted through his fingers.

Janeia snapped, "Fuck!"

The Whale's eyes grew wider as Molasses fired his second shot through the man's forehead, slamming him into the wall.

Theessrrpp!

Bloom!

He fired a third shot into the man's heart.

Theessrrpp!

The Whale slid to the floor with his last breath.

Janeia continued struggling to break free, but Molasses pulled her into him and stared her down. No words were needed. She got the message. *Keep your mouth shut and stay calm!*

Molasses wiped his fingerprints from the silencer gun with the sheets, and slipped the gun back into his black leather carrying bag. He then led Janeia toward the door.

BACK outside in the parking lot of the hotel, Molasses and Janeia calmly walked to the dark sedan.

Janeia was still shocked and in need of plenty of answers.

"What happened to the Lincoln?" she asked him first.

"Obviously, somebody stole it. Now get in," Molasses told her. They had no time for small talk. He helped her into the passenger side of the sedan and shut the door behind her.

Janeia shut her mouth as Molasses climbed behind the wheel on the driver's side. He dropped the black leather carrying bag to the ground beside the car and drove off.

Shortly after, Charlie drove back around to the parking lot in the Lincoln and retrieved the carrying bag from the ground.

•••

JANEIA stared into empty space as Molasses drove north on Interstate 55. He was headed back to Chicago.

Janeia didn't know what to say to him. What the hell was going on? Was killing people Molasses's business? Was that what the trip to St. Louis was all about? And why would he take her along with him?

Molasses finally decided to break the silence.

"Are you all right?" he asked her.

He knew that she would be. He selected his women carefully. If they seemed too easily shaken, or ran their fucking mouth more than they needed to, he chose not to deal with them.

Janeia responded to him with hesitation.

"I can talk now?"

Molasses stared at her for a minute. She seemed more obedient than he had first assessed.

"Say what's on your mind," he told her.

She nodded to him slowly.

"Okay." She took a deep breath before she started. "Is this your idea of a 'business trip'?"

Molasses was cool as the breeze. He knew what kind of woman Janeia was. She could take what he had to tell her.

He looked her in the eyes and answered, "Yes. I kill people for a living. But mostly bad people. That's my first rule."

Janeia took the first blow, swallowed hard, sucked in another breath, and regained her composure.

She said, "You have *rules* . . . for killing people?"

Molasses raised his open right hand.

"Five of 'em," he told her.

She was curious, and it would be a long car drive back to Chicago. So she asked him, "Which are?"

Molasses ran it all down to her.

"Number one, if you got it coming to you anyway, and the price is right, then I'll be the one to do it. And that fat-ass back there had plenty of people who wanted him dead . . . including his wife."

Janeia listened, taking it all in.

"And number two?" she asked him.

Molasses looked into her eyes again. He had chosen her well. The chick was attempting to understand his world.

He explained, "I want half my money up front, and the other half after the job. And I want no fucking excuses. Because if I don't get paid . . . somebody's falling, and they ain't getting up."

Janeia found it hard not to smile. Molasses had personality.

"Okay? What else?" she asked him.

He continued, "Number three . . . I execute all clean jobs. I don't like no sloppy shit. And that includes number four . . ."

He stared at her intently.

". . . no fucking witnesses. So you didn't *see* shit, and you didn't *hear* shit. Because if you did . . . if you even *think* you did . . . then I gotta lay you down. And it's nothing personal. It's just business."

Janeia nodded to him.

"And number five?"

Molasses answered, "My last rule . . . is no killing women . . . and no children."

Janeia thought it over logically.

She said, "What if a woman decided to be a witness?" She was just being curious again. She wasn't the type to drop a dime on her man. And Molasses knew it.

He finally looked away when he answered her.

"Then God help her. And God help me."

Janeia sat in silence for a minute. She was letting it all sink in. She looked into his steady, dark brown face and wanted to know more.

"So how did you . . . start off doing this?"

Molasses studied her eyes again. She was taking it farther than he expected.

"You really wanna know?"

Janeia nodded to him with no hesitation.

"Yeah."

Molasses grinned and nodded back. The chick was really feeling him. He had been dying to tell his story to some-body. And since they had plenty of time on their hands, he decided to tell her a few dark things about himself, just in case he never got the chance again.

"Growing up on the West Side of Chicago, it seemed like every day some new asshole wanted to test you," he told her. "And then in high school . . . somebody finally went and killed my boy over some petty shit. And the badass who did it . . . nobody liked him. So when I found him and got his ass back . . . nobody cared."

Janeia listened to him and didn't flinch. She wanted to understand it. She wanted to be down for him. She wanted to open herself up for what he had to say for himself. Everyone had a story, and she wanted to hear his.

"And then you just started . . . killing people for pay?"

Molasses shook off the simplicity of her logic. His situa-tion was a lot more complicated than that.

He answered, "Naw, that was just love for my boy. The *second* time was what did it. Another one of them thug types wanted another notch on his belt . . . I guess. So he starts telling everybody that 'Moe 'bout to take a dive.' I didn't want to be no killing machine, Janeia. God knows I didn't. So I just laid low. But you know how niggas are. This moth-erfucker came looking for me."

Molasses became animated in telling his story.

" 'It's time for *war*! It's time for *war*!' So what was I supposed to do? Lay down my life for some cowboy-and-Indian shit?" he asked her.

"Hell no!" he answered emphatically. "So he found what he was looking for . . . and he turned up MIA."

Molasses paused for a beat to calm himself behind the wheel.

"And after that," he told her, "people just started bringing their personal dramas to me. 'Yo, Moe, man, homeboy ain't right. I just wish he would go away somewhere. You hear what I'm saying? Even if I had to *pay* somebody to do it.' "

Molasses stopped and looked deeply into Janeia's eyes before he continued.

"So I asked, 'How much you thinkin' 'bout paying?' "

Janeia was all ears, feeling every part of his story.

Molasses looked away again with his conclusion.

"I'm not trying to say that it's right. I'm just saying that's how I'm living right now."

After he told me how he lives his life . . .
I could either take it . . . or
leave it . . . and I chose to take it.

As Molasses continued to drive up Interstate 55 toward
Chicago, Janeia placed her left hand on his right thigh.
She began to feel comfortable with him again, more comfortable than before. He had shared with her the raw
truth of his lifestyle, and she could take it. That was what
he wanted from her, her total dedication to him with no
lies between them. So he looked into her eyes and face
with warmth and pride, like a wolf who cared for its
young.

MONDAY morning at Chicago State University, new students and upperclassmen headed to class and hung out on
the campus grounds.

Inside the school cafeteria, Janeia sat at a table eating
lunch with her main girlfriend, Brenda, the one she told
most of her personal shit to.

Brenda talked through a mouthful of tuna fish sandwich.

"So, what's up with this new guy you've been seeing? Do
tell."

Janeia smiled at her, a turkey breast sandwich in hand.

"He's not the kind of man I can talk about like that," she
answered.

Brenda stopped eating for a minute to stare. She was concerned for her girl.

"What is he, another hustler? Girl, you gotta stop dealing with those kind of guys. Seriously!"

Janeia blew her off.

"He's not a hustler."

"So what does he do then?"

Janeia shook her head and refused to speak on it.

Brenda decided to press her.

"I mean, come on, how bad is he?"

Janeia told her, "You don't wanna know. And I mean that."

Brenda paused for a second.

"Girl, do you realize that your name is a damn oxymoron? Because there is nothing *Goode* about you. You just seem to care about all the wrong kinds of people."

Brenda returned to eating her lunch.

Janeia thought about her friend's comments and decided to defend her character.

"Well, at least I *know* he's bad. He's *honest* about it. Not like some of these guys who fake it. None of these guys out here are as good as they claim to be anyway. So I'd rather have the truth than that bullshit."

Chi-Town hustler and part-time student Dollar Bill approached their table right on cue. Big jewelry and street-life glitter was all around him from his sideways Chicago Cubs baseball hat down to his straight-out-of-the-box Timberland boots.

"What's up, Janeia? I heard you not fucking with that nigga Chase no more. So what's up now, you a free woman again?"

Dollar Bill took an uninvited seat at their table. Janeia looked to Brenda, who grunted and looked away. Those thug niggas had a lot of nerve.

Janeia asked him, "Why do you even bother to show up here? I mean, it's obvious you don't go to any classes."

Brenda laughed at it. Dollar Bill eyeballed her for a second and then looked back to Janeia. Fuck wasting time with Brenda. She wasn't a dime piece like Janeia was.

He then admitted his fetish for schoolgirls.

"Shit, are you crazy? All the baddest bitches are up in here. Girls who got jobs and are moving up in the world but are still down with the streets. Like you, Janeia. I always dug your game on that."

Brenda gave Janeia a look and grinned. She was just trying to tell her girl the same shit before the hustler walked up on them.

Janeia sighed and returned Brenda's lingering stare.

She said, "You ever feel like you need a long-ass vacation somewhere? *Anywhere.*"

Brenda nodded to her.

"Every day of my life."

Dollar Bill added his own opinion.

"You don't need a damn vacation. You need a thug in your life, wit' a stiff dick in you."

Adding insult to injury, he told Brenda, "You soft, bitch. You need to take lessons from Janeia. She *knows* what time it is out here. Right, Janeia?"

Janeia ignored him and was embarrassed by it. But the boy was right. She *did* know what time it was in the streets, whether that street knowledge was healthy for her or not.

He said, "I'm gon' have my turn in a minute. It's gon' be me and you next."

Janeia piped, "In your fuckin' wet *dreams!*"

He said, "I don't have those no more. I get plenty of panties now. And I'm gon' get a pair of yours, too, Janeia. That's a promise."

He stood up to leave with a grin across his sinister brown face.

Brenda looked into Janeia's eyes after Dollar Bill left, and she was filled with pity for her. The thug life was hardly glamorous. And all of the flashy videos of the hard-knocks streets sold nothing but illusions, while masking the pain wrapped in marketable, urban hipness.

INSIDE her psychology class that afternoon, Janeia sat at her desk and daydreamed while a middle-aged and graying white professor spoke at the large blackboard at the front of the room. He held chalk in his hand as he wrote key points from his lecture onto the blackboard.

"The *id* is known as our unconscious and psychic energy to satisfy our instinctual drives for survival, such as hunger, thirst, sex, and basic aggression.

"The id operates on the *pleasure principle*, and seeks immediate gratification that is totally unconstrained by reality. . . ."

I'm in my junior year of college, studying psychology, of all things. . . . But if you ask me, I would say that my life is rather boring. So I imagined what Molasses's life was like . . . out on the streets.

Brooklyn, New York.

Molasses drove across the Brooklyn Bridge from Manhattan in another dark sedan rental car. He studied his detailed navigation-system map from a laptop computer that sat open on the passenger seat. He wanted to make sure he didn't waste any time getting lost.

When he reached his destination in the Italian section of Brooklyn, he sat patiently inside the car at the corner, with a clear view of an Italian hangout in the middle of the block.

Inside the dark, smoky tavern, connected mafia men and wannabes stood at the bar, smoking, drinking, and enjoying small talk.

A young, slick-haired wiseguy sat at the bar enjoying a drink himself. But he looked as if the weight of the world was riding on the slim shoulders of his dark, tailored suit. An older, gray-haired wiseguy sat beside him with a lot more poise. He looked more relaxed and comfortable sitting in his broad-shouldered suit.

Out on the street, Molasses continued to watch and wait

from inside the dark sedan. He had parked across the street and at the far corner, diagonally from the tavern. It was a perfect view for a killer.

Inside the car, Molasses turned off the navigation system, closed the laptop computer, and pulled out his silencer gun with a scope attached. He placed the gun on the floor between his legs and kept his cool.

Back inside the tavern, the young wiseguy, known as The Kid, was growing restless.

"I'm stepping outside to take a smoke," he told the old head.

The old head grimaced.

"For what? Everybody smokes in here. This isn't The Garden, with the goddamned smoking police harassing you. What's the matter wit' you?"

Around the Italian tavern, it looked like every customer in the joint was smoking. So what was the fucking reason for walking outside?

"I just need some fresh air," The Kid commented. So he got up and walked. He strolled right out the door and away from safety, and stood in front of the tavern's window, giving a clear view to his flat, olive-toned forehead.

Inside the rental car at the corner, Molasses saw The Kid, and he immediately reached for the gun on the floor between his legs.

He smiled and shook his head, talking to himself in the car.

"You gotta be bullshittin' me."

How easy could it be to kill a young sleepwalker who was out to lunch on his safety? Molasses expected to sit in that car and wait for his mark for a couple of days if he had to. But the job was being given to him on a silver platter in a mere thirty minutes.

So he checked his surroundings for witnesses, raised his

silencer gun, used his scope vision, and cracked the window just enough to shoot.

The older wiseguy walked out of the tavern just in time to step right in the way.

That pissed Molasses the fuck off.

"Shit!" he cursed to himself.

It wasn't going to be that simple a job after all.

Outside, the older man looked around and asked The Kid, "Are you all right out here?"

The young man seemed irritated by him even asking. He figured he could take care of himself. He was twenty-seven years old for God's sake. He wasn't a teenager afraid of a busted lip and a bloody nose anymore.

That was just what the wiser man was afraid of. Once you grow up and become a member of the organization, you would rarely get a busted lip or a bloody nose anymore. You'd get a busted head and a bloody chest, neither of which could be healed with an ice bag.

Nevertheless, a young fool would always find a way to *be* a fool. So The Kid ran his mouth to declare his independence.

"Jesus Christ, Al! Would you stop it with the fuckin' babysitting already? I'm just getting some air out here."

The older wiseguy nodded to him. He didn't like it. He knew better. But he was once young and stupid himself. And *he* survived his own brash stupidity to reach old age. So maybe he was overreacting.

He agreed, grudgingly, to let The Kid get some fresh air out on his own.

"All right."

Before the older man walked back inside, he took another look around on instincts and spotted nothing that stood out to him. So he walked back into to the bar.

Inside the dark sedan at the corner, Molasses reestablished his aim with the scope vision. He held steady and took one good shot.

Theessrrpp!

Bull's-eye! The bullet connected near the temple. The Kid fell to the ground and was dead instantly.

Molasses quickly pulled his gun down, restarted his car, and drove off. By the time the old wiseguy walked back out of the smoky tavern and found The Kid shot and bleeding on the ground, Molasses was already three blocks away.

He told me that a lot of hits were simple . . . but others were more complicated.

Los Angeles, California.

At a crowded urban playground, excited kids, West Coast gangbangers, and proud hotties in skimpy summertime outfits were everywhere. West Coast chicks with long braided hair and long fingernails watched and talked shit from the bleachers as young and old Crips and Bloods in their respective blue and red colors ran a heated game of basketball for money and neighborhood bragging rights. It was a new form of competition between the sets.

Short Blood, an undersized and quick ball handler for the red squad, was also quick with the lips, and he was talking plenty of shit.

"They ain't got nobody who can stick me. I'm toastin' fools. *Toastin'* 'em!"

He made it to the basket behind some nifty moves only to have his shot blocked by a much taller Crip on the blue squad.

The tall Crip talked smack right back to him.

"Get that shit outta here. You gotta pay a *toll* down here, nigga! I want ten *duckets* for every shot."

Molasses showed up at their playground wearing a neutral, light gray jogging suit with white-on-white basketball shoes. He carried a medium-size sports bag with him, packed with a change of clothes, a couple of white hotel towels, a big bottle of Gatorade, and his gun in a special compartment. He sat down real easily at the edge of the bleachers and surveyed the crowded scene. It was important for him to look as normal as possible even while knowing that *they knew* he was not one of them.

So Molasses passed himself off as a visiting sports jock who was more than happy to watch them run ball.

He watched as Short Blood pulled up for a long three-point shot behind the foul-line circle and hit nothing but the bottom of the net.

Molasses responded to it with an overzealous smile.

"Got' damn!"

Short Blood was ready to talk his shit again.

"Take *them* ten duckets!" he shouted at the tall Crip who had blocked his shot earlier.

Trouble Red, a Blood O.G., pulled out a wad of cash to begin betting on the game. He had good size, a solid build, and a pleasant brown face.

He reached out and stretched five twenties across the ground.

"I got all the duckets you need right here. Now, who talking to me?"

Molasses watched him and recognized his mark. He nodded to himself. He realized that he may have to wait awhile.

As Trouble Red began to take bets with the ball game still in progress, a hot, young L.A. chick walked up on him and offered the Blood a sure bet that he couldn't refuse, her naked, chestnut brown wetness.

The girl looked no older than seventeen. But her body was all the way mature, peeking like an exotic mountain through her curve-accentuating clothes.

"Got' damn! Stop the game for the halftime show!"

someone shouted out of the crowd of spectators in reference to the young hottie.

They all laughed while the girl continued to give Trouble Red a perfect view of her well-rounded ass, tucked away
in tight blue jeans.

She smiled and said, "Hey, Red. I got the house to myself
until late. What's up like that?"

The young chick was taking the bold approach to getting
her shit off. She figured the quicker she got him to the crib,
the longer he could turn her hot ass out.

The loud spectator overheard the girl's comments to the
Blood, and he decided to add to it with more humor.

"She said she got the house to herself, like, *whoa*! That's
crazy, Red. What you gon' do?"

They all laughed again on and off the courts.

Molasses smiled at the comedian his damn self.

He even mumbled to himself from the bleachers, "Gon'
on, girl. Lead him out of here."

She would make his job a hell of a lot easier. Catching a
man in the act of a good screw was priceless.

But Trouble Red blew the young girl off. Ever since he
gave her a taste of his raw steel a few months ago, the young
chick was like a reckless crackhead begging for another shot
of his strong pelvic thrusts.

"Come on, girl. I got money to get up out here," he told her.

Just then the tall Crip with the shot-blocking skills threw
down a monster slam dunk to end the game.

Trouble Red painfully watched his money walk away in
Crip hands.

"Shit!" he cursed himself. Then he took another look at
the young girl's ripe ass. "Aw'ight, let's go."

The loudmouthed spectator was at it again.

He said, "If you ask me, you da one who won the bet,
Red. 'Cause I'd take some of that ass *for sho'*!"

Molasses couldn't tell if the guy was Blood or Crip. He wore neither colors in his white tee and beige khakis. So maybe he was just a crazy-ass neutral nigga who the affiliated bangers ignored.

However, Trouble Red grew tired of his mouth and snapped at him.

"Ay, watch your fuckin' mouth, man! Ain't nobody ask you shit out here. You still want your damn tongue, nigga?"

The loud spectator looked nervous and backed his loud ass down.

"Yes, sir. I'm sorry."

"Yeah, you *gon'* be sorry. You keep running your damn mouth so much," Trouble Red warned him.

His young chick noticed his blood pressure rising to action levels. So she moved to calm him down before he hauled off and used his pistol out there.

She placed her long, painted nails gently on his muscular arm and said, "Hey, don't waste your energy on that nigga. Save it for me. 'Cause I got something just for you."

Trouble Red looked her over again and nodded to her with a smile. And they walked away from the basketball courts together.

Molasses watched them and grinned from the bleachers. It was a perfect setup. He took a look around to survey who was watching him to make sure his cover was clear. Then he stood up and slipped away behind them.

BY the time the sun went down that evening in L.A., Trouble Red was half naked and sweaty, while enjoying a doggy-style spanking of his young sex addict in her small room.

"*Oooh, yeeaah! Oooh, bay-beeee,*" the girl moaned. She had her hands placed out forward on the carpeted floor, with her knees tucked in, and her ass up and spread.

Trouble Red was pounding into her from behind like a

jackhammer. He gripped her smooth, brown hips to lever-
age his force.

OUTSIDE the West Coast–style flat, Molasses found it
rather easy to creep inside. There were a number of win-
dows that were cracked open for ventilation. And they were
all at ground level with no bars on them. How easy could
that be?

Back inside the girl's dark, hot room, Trouble Red was so
filled with bliss that he didn't notice Molasses sneak up at
the doorway and begin to watch them. He cracked the door
open just enough to get a good look.

After a few minutes of scoping out the show, Molasses
decided to give himself away with a laugh.

Trouble Red immediately turned to face him in alarm.

"What the fuck . . . ?"

Molasses already had his black silencer in hand.

He said, "Go ahead and finish your nut, Red. I don't
wanna ruin your last one. That would be wrong. I mean, I
wouldn't want you to do that shit to me."

Trouble Red disengaged from the girl and questioned
her betrayal.

"Who the fuck is he?"

The girl looked confused and bashful. She moved to
grab the sheets from her bed to cover up her naked body.

She answered, "I don't know him."

Trouble Red was still skeptical.

"Bitch, you set me the fuck up!" he shouted at her. He
moved to tuck his dick back into his pants, but couldn't do
it. He was still rock hard.

The girl whined at his accusation. She was innocent.

She said, "I did not. I wouldn't do that to you. I don't
know him."

Molasses decided to help her out.

He said, "She has nothing to do with this, Red. But you got a whole lot of enemies bidding on your life. I hear you need to learn how to control that temper of yours."

Trouble Red told him the hell off, despite the silencer gun that Molasses cradled in his hands.

"Man, fuck you!"

Molasses looked him over and calmly shook his head.

"See what I mean? You don't even know me. And you in here talking shit while I got a gun in my hand," he told the angry Blood.

Trouble Red asked him defiantly, "So what'chu gon' do, stare at my dick? Or you came in here to do somethin'?"

The girl tried to move over toward the bed to reach for her clothes. Molasses waved the gun at her to stop.

"Get back to where you were. I like that view from here. And take them sheets back off."

The girl had no choice but to obey him. She dropped the sheets from her naked body, revealing the sweetest brown curves that two eager eyes could ever see.

Molasses shook his head again and smiled.

He told the Blood, "Damn. You sure went out with a good one, man."

Trouble Red was so pissed off that he jumped at the gun, like a panther in the night. However, Molasses expected as much. So he was forced to fire on the Blood before he wanted to. He wanted to toy with him just a little bit longer.

Trouble Red took the first bullet through the palm of his left hand.

Theessrrpp!

"*Ahhh!*" he screamed.

A second bullet ripped through his shoulder, knocking him backward.

Theessrrpp!

And a third bullet met with his forehead.

Theessrrpp!

He fell dead on the girl's carpeted floor.

The girl screamed in vain. It was a little too late for that. Her lover was already greeting the devils and demons in hell.

Molasses told her, "Now you know we don't need all that. You know the rules. You a big girl now, up in here fucking gangsters doggy style when your momma ain't home. You know that ain't right. So shut your damn mouth. And you lucky I don't kill no women and kids. So you didn't *hear* me and you didn't *see* me. Right?"

Molasses looked at her with steely eyes, while still holding his silencer in hand.

The naked girl was slow to respond. She was in a daze. She just couldn't believe what was happening.

Molasses continued to stare at her with his gun.

"You think you saw or heard something?" he quizzed her.

The girl finally shook her head with tears in her eyes.

"No," she mumbled.

"That's what I thought," he told her. "So I'll drag the body out of here, and you clean up the blood."

Molasses reached to grab Trouble Red's dead body by the legs, and pulled it toward the window.

The girl finally gathered her clothes and proceeded to wipe her tears away. Then she looked down at the blood of her lover that had been shed across the carpet at her feet.

It's amazing what one can get away with in the absence of fear. Molasses pulled a dead man's body into the trunk of his dark sedan with urgency and went unnoticed. Imagine that. But if he had hesitated for even a second, he would have been busted by neighborhood onlookers.

As far as what the girl would say about Trouble Red's missing body . . . that was all on her. She shouldn't have gotten herself so deeply involved with dangerous niggas.

*And he told me that . . .
sometimes . . . things just got
downright sloppy.*

Molasses's flight touched down at the Dallas /Fort Worth International Airport right on schedule. When the plane rolled up to the gate and stopped, he gathered his lone black carry-on bag in his left hand and held the *USA Today* newspaper he had been reading in his right. He was dressed in a tailored dark suit, with a white dress shirt and a conservative tie, like a legitimate businessman. And when he walked confidently through the airport terminal toward the baggage claim and ground travel, he caught many respectful stares from the other travelers. In their minds, he appeared to be a clean-cut, Wall Street brother. But the reality of his profession was nothing to be proud of.

Molasses walked outside of the airport on a sunny Texas day and stood at the taxi booth. A taxi pulled up for him immediately. He hopped in and gave the driver the name of his hotel.

"The Marriott on the north end."

The East Indian taxi driver nodded to him and sped off toward the airport terminal exit without speaking a word.

THAT afternoon in the parking lot of a suburban Texas mall, Molasses approached a white Ford Taurus rental car.

The door was unlocked and the keys were inside.

Molasses stared at the white Taurus and frowned.

He mumbled, "Shit! You couldn't find anything better than *white*?"

His young white business partner, Charlie, watched him from a dark sedan in the distance of the parking lot. He made his usual cell phone call for the setup.

Molasses climbed inside the rental car and answered the ringing cell phone that had been locked inside the glove compartment.

"Is Mr. Brown around?" he asked Charlie over the line.

Charlie answered, "He certainly is."

He then climbed out of his sedan and started walking toward the busy mall entrance. They had a movie theater inside that he wanted to visit. He figured he'd catch a comedy flick while Molasses did his work.

"And you sure that this is a simple house call?" Molasses quizzed him.

"That's what it is," Charlie answered.

Molasses nodded with the phone to his ear and thought no more of it.

"We'll talk about it later."

He hung up the phone and pulled out the laptop computer for his navigation system. He keyed in the shortest route to Mr. Brown's home in suburban Dallas. He then checked the floor of the backseat to make sure his silencer bag was inside. It was.

IN an exotic, upper-class housing development of four- and five-bedroom homes, with wide green lawns in suburban Dallas, all was quiet, safe, and sound. It was like a painting, where nothing moved.

Molasses pulled up to park at Mr. Brown's place in his white Taurus rental car, immediately disturbing the neighborhood painting. This place didn't get many visitors, and in a white rental car with a briefcase in the middle of the day, Molasses looked like a well-dressed salesman.

He slipped his silencer gun under his *USA Today* newspaper and held it perfectly folded to conceal the weapon. He then grabbed his briefcase.

He climbed out of the rental and walked up to Mr. Brown's front door with his briefcase in his right hand and his folded newspaper in the left. Once he arrived, he calmly rang the doorbell.

A middle-aged and balding black man showed up from behind the large wooden door and looked out through the side window. He noticed the white rental car parked at the curb, and he shook his head without even looking at Molasses good. He responded to the stranger at his door with heated irritation.

He opened the door just to give the well-mannered salesman a piece of his mind.

"Look, man, what the hell are you selling? Don't you know that this is a no-solicitation neighborhood here?"

Molasses addressed him cool and calm.

"Not even for a good old American murder?"

Mr. Brown's eyes grew wide right before Molasses shot him three times with the silencer gun in his left hand instead of his right. What the hell, he was too close to miss. With the job easily done, Molasses politely closed the man's front door and walked away, leaving Mr. Brown freshly murdered behind his doorway.

But before Molasses could make it back to his rental car and leave the scene as smoothly as he had entered, an athletic white man taking an afternoon jog spotted him. The man was jogging with a black poodle at his side, who took the liberty to bark his miniature mouth at Molasses. The dark brown man was an obvious intruder to the neighborhood.

Molasses met eyes with the white man and remained calm. His instincts told him everything he needed to know. Many American white men were still terrified of dark-skinned strangers. And Molasses could read fear like a hound dog could sniff blood.

Nevertheless, he played the white man softly.

"How are you doing?" he asked. "It's a pretty nice day out today, isn't it?"

The jogger nodded to him suspiciously.

"Yeah, it is," he answered.

However, the curly-haired black poodle wasn't as cordial. He continued to bark his little ass off.

"Arrk, arrk, arrk, arrk!"

Molasses began to worry about his newspaper and the gun. He wondered if the dog was familiar with the smell of gunpowder. He wouldn't put it past him. Wealthy white men loved to hunt with their dogs. Especially in the South where they had more land and game to hunt.

So the jogger continued to look Molasses over, questions obviously on his mind.

"Are you a salesman?" he went ahead and asked.

Molasses responded, "Nah, I'm just a friend of the family. I was visiting for a lunch break."

The jogger remained suspicious, but he decided to let it slide for the moment.

"Oh yeah. Well, have a nice visit," he offered.

Molasses climbed back into his rental car and was disappointed. He realized that the job was now not as easy as Charlie had thought. And that damn dog was still barking as he ignited the engine.

As soon as Molasses drove out of sight, the skeptical jogger headed back home with his dog. Once there, he immediately locked his door and stepped up to the kitchen phone. He just had a bad feeling about the black man in his bones. Wealthy white men tended to have those feelings whenever strange black men showed up unannounced in their well-to-do neighborhoods. Skepticism was a normal feeling for many of them.

So he made a quick phone call over to Mr. Brown's house to shoot the breeze with him, and to indirectly ask about the afternoon visitor to his house that day.

But over at Mr. Brown's house, when the telephone rang, he was unable to answer the call. He was lying dead in a pool of blood in the front entrance foyer.

Back at the jogger's house, the man began to panic as the phone continued to ring with no answer.

In a back room, his dog began to bark before suddenly going silent.

Without pause, the man hung up the call to Mr. Brown's place and began to dial 9-1-1. He got to the first "1" when Molasses appeared and shoved him away from the phone.

He looked at Molasses in a state of shock.

"What exactly are you doing here?" he asked defiantly. The man was attempting to mask his fear with anger.

Molasses didn't buy it. He slowly revealed his gun.

He said, "You know what, my friend? You just happened to be in the wrong place at the wrong damn time."

The white man began to fidget. The courageous game was over. He now feared for his life.

He said, "You know, you just can't go around killing people. That's just not right. You just can't do that."

He was assuming things correctly.

However, Molasses played it off. He looked at the man in confusion.

"Who said I killed someone? Did you see me kill anyone?" he asked the jogger civilly.

"Well, what are you doing with the gun? And how did you get into my home?" the white man asked him. He began to call for his dog. "Puff-fee? . . . Puff-fee?"

Molasses thought about the dog.

He said, "Can I ask you a question?"

"Yes," the man responded.

"How come you white folks always choose to have a little *black* dog?" Molasses quizzed him. He was just curious about the mentality of the shit. Did the white man still have a craving for the color black to be subservient to him?

The jogger seemed embarrassed by the question.

He answered, "I assure you, it has absolutely *nothing* to do with race."

Molasses responded to him with a straight face.

"Yeah, well, *Puffy* had a big-ass mouth. So I had to *close* it for him. And now it looks like I gotta close yours."

The man backed up in horror and attempted to run away while screaming for his life.

"*Hellllp* . . ."

His sudden outburst forced Molasses to fire several shots into the man's back and head as he tried to escape his fate.

Theessrrpp! Theessrrpp! Theessrrpp!

Molasses moved to the broken back door that he'd shot off and stepped over the dog he'd killed upon his entry. He hurried out of the man's house and climbed back into the rental car to drive off.

MOLASSES took a couple of deep breaths and shook his head as he drove away from the upscale neighborhood. He was obviously not immune to fear. The incident had him shaken. But it was nothing that he couldn't handle. Emotions simply proved that he was still alive.

He pulled the cell phone out of the glove compartment and called Charlie; he had a few heated words for him.

Charlie answered his cell. He was sitting in an empty, dark movie theater where he was enjoying a comedy with a bag of popcorn.

"Hello," he answered with a chuckle from the humorous antics of the film.

"Fuck is so funny to you?" Molasses snapped at him. There wasn't a comedy being shown on his end of town.

Charlie stopped smiling and eating his popcorn and responded with concern.

"What happened? Is everything okay?"

Molasses was still peppered inside the rental car.

He said, "I thought you told me this was an easy sell in a secluded neighborhood."

Charlie repeated his question of concern.

"Well, what happened? You set off a fire alarm?"

"Nah, I got the new mailman treatment," Molasses answered.

Charlie began to chuckle a minute.

"Oh, yeah?" But then he regained his seriousness. "So . . . what did you do?"

Molasses responded cool and calm again.

He said, "I'm a businessman. So I handled my business. But you owe me one, Charlie. You hear me? You owe me one."

Charlie whined to him.

"Look, I can't control that kind of thing."

Molasses cut him off.

"I don't give a fuck, man! You know how I like things. So you owe me one. It's as simple as that," he told him.

Charlie backed down and agreed to it.

"All right, all right. I owe you one."

He hung up his cell phone in the dark theater and shook his head. The hit-man business paid well, but the shit was a real hassle sometimes, like any other high-priced hustle.

The conflict had spoiled the charm of the movie.

"Damn dogs," Charlie mumbled to himself. And since he was no longer feeling humorous with a you-owe-me-one hanging over his head from a demanding hit man, he stood up to leave and left his popcorn on the chair.

A FEW days later at Molasses's condo on the southeast side of Chicago, the red, cordless telephone on his kitchen wall rang.

Molasses hurried from his guest bathroom to answer it. He wore only a white towel around his waist and slippers. He had taken an afternoon shower, and his hair and body were still wet.

"Yeah," he answered.

He immediately frowned when he heard the familiar jagged voice of an older woman. His mother.

"I need some money," she told him. "And learn how to answer your phone correctly. I never taught you how to say *hello*?"

Molasses shook his head.

"I love you, too, Mom. And I'm doing just fine in my life," he responded sarcastically. "How's your life doing?"

In the backyard in a Chicago suburb, Molasses's mother was dressed in a jazzy, dark blue skirt suit. She was an attractive black woman in her early fifties who still looked high-maintenance. She sat in her backyard deck chair overlooking the dark green lawn. She had an expensive, multi-channel cordless telephone in hand, holding it with French-manicured nails.

"My life could be a lot damn better. That's why I need some money," she answered her only son.

"How much you need this time?" he asked her.

She stared at the phone for a second. Was he patronizing her?

"Warren, who the hell are you talkin' to, boy?" she asked him back.

He refused to back down from her. He was a grown-ass man now.

He said, "Obviously you think I'm some kind of a damn bank."

She snapped, "Well, if you feel that way, then don't give it to me."

Back at Molasses's condo, he continued to shake his head in disbelief. What was he going to do about his mother? She remained an insatiable woman.

He said, "I'll wire you whatever you need in an hour."

His mother immediately cheered up over the line, like a giddy high school girl.

"Oh, thank you, baby. I need that. And oh, I love you, too."

"So how much do you need?" he asked her again.

His mother paused before she responded, "Three thousand."

Molasses smiled to himself.

"Aw'ight," he mumbled.

He hung the phone up with his mother and went on about his business. She couldn't help herself. She was who she was, and he was who *he* was. So he placed the cordless phone back on its wall-mounted charger and returned to the bathroom. He had to finish getting ready for his hot date on the Chicago town that night.

*Then he would make time for me.
And I must admit . . . his perks definitely
made an impression on me.*

Molasses walked through his elaborate condominium apartment and entered a long walk-in closet that was filled with fine suits, slacks, shirts, and shoes.

He pulled out a dark brown suit, brown alligator shoes, and another eggshell-colored silk shirt with no tie. When he was all dressed, patted down with Armani cologne, and ready to split, he walked down into the connected garage at the bottom level and opened up a dark brown Bentley Arnage convertible with an automatic key ring. A black Navigator was parked right beside it.

Molasses climbed inside the tan leather interior of the Bentley, pressed the garage door button that was inside the car, and said hello to the bright Chicago sunshine as the garage door lifted open.

Molasses drove out of the garage along Lakeshore Drive on Chicago's East Side, loving the spoils of his dangerous profession.

He looked like a black prince, driving behind a royal chariot along urban terrain. Who the hell *wouldn't* be attracted to that black man? Molasses had the street game on lock, and he *knew* it!

•••

JANEIA Goode stood patiently on 83rd Street near her South Side Chicago home waiting for Molasses to pick her up. It was the same street where she had met him a few months ago, while on her way to school. But she hadn't been able to spend a great deal of time with him since then, so she looked forward to every chance she got.

Molasses drove up the block and pulled over to the curb in front of her in his Bentley. His arrival brought a huge smile to her face. The eager college girl could not even disguise it. He was the kind of hard-core, money-having nigga that the new wave of urban girls dreamed about. And he could *fuck*, too. What more could a young needful chick ask for in a man?

However, as she climbed into the plush ride, a curious older cop watched her from his parked police cruiser up the street. He was a black man from the 'hood himself who knew better. Average cats didn't drive Bentleys, and Molasses didn't play for the Bulls, Bears, Cubs, White Sox or produce hot love songs with R. Kelly. So what was he into? He looked too tailored for rap music. Another high-priced game rocked his boat.

Inside the police cruiser, the forty-something black officer had a cell phone that rang from the cup holder where it sat near his dashboard. He read the phone number of his home phone. It was his wife calling him for the third time that day.

He answered it with irritation as he watched the Bentley with the mysterious younger brother at the wheel.

"Yeah, honey," the black cop answered. His badge read L. Barrett.

He listened to his wife ranting about dance lessons for their eight-year-old daughter before he finally decided to respond to her.

"Honey, I've already been working overtime to send her

to the school that she's in now. I can't pay for this other thing. We still have to eat."

He listened to his wife's rebuttal and responded again.

"Well, some people can afford those extra luxuries. But we just can't do it right now, baby. She's just gonna have to learn that she can't have everything she wants when she wants it."

He continued to watch the scene as Molasses drove right past his police cruiser. Officer Barrett looked him over for next time and made sure to glance at the license plate number.

INSIDE the Bentley, Janeia was enjoying the hell out of herself. What a sweet dream of a ride it was. She reclined in her seat and continued to smile. She was dressed to impress herself in a sheer, burgundy dress.

She looked over and told Molasses, "Well, you look nice tonight. Smell good, too."

Molasses grinned at her.

He said, "Oh, likewise." Then he took a sniff of her. "On both counts," he added.

Janeia smacked his right shoulder playfully.

"Have you had a nice day?" she asked him.

Molasses grimaced.

"My mom called me asking for money, as always, but it's been a peaceful day outside of that."

Janeia hesitated to ask her next question. Then she decided that she would.

"So . . . does that mean you didn't have to kill anyone today?"

Molasses was thoughtful. He needed to give her a clearer view of his profession. Or at least on *his* level.

He answered, "Nah, you got the wrong idea. It's not like taking out the trash every day. It's more like . . . a jazz musician, who only plays his music every once in a blue moon.

"And he gets paid *well* for it, so he can choose to play whenever he wants to," he added.

Janeia looked him in his eyes.

"Can he decide not to play at all?"

She figured it was worth a shot to at least ask.

Molasses looked away from her. Chicks were forever trying to change a man's game. But since she had the courage to ask, he decided to give her the truth on the matter.

"He thinks about it all the time," he told her. Then he looked back into her eyes to lead her away from the subject.

"But look, I don't want to think about that shit when I'm out with you. I showed you what I do so that we would have no confusion about it. I didn't want to be ducking and hiding shit from you," he told her. "But I don't want to talk about that shit all the time either. So just be a woman for me right now and look pretty for me . . . and love me."

He broke her down into a warm smile.

She said, "Okay. I think I can do that."

She placed her hand on his right thigh and stared at him. She looked touched by heaven, even while being courted from hell.

Molasses asked her softly, "So what time should I have you back at home tonight?"

She grinned at him and answered, "Eight . . . tomorrow morning."

Molasses smiled back and squeezed her thigh.

He said, "I think I can do that. What you got, early classes tomorrow?"

She nodded to him.

"Yeah."

THAT evening at The Grand, a five-star Chicago hotel, Molasses and his young lady stepped out of the Bentley in

front of the valet booth. The valets were damn-near salivat-
ing to park his Bentley. Not only would it be a pleasure to
drive, but what would the *tip* be from the owner?

Molasses smiled, reading their eager stares—normal
behavior for those who would never be privileged enough
to own the expensive luxury car.

"Just don't scratch it. Or that's your life," he joked to
them.

They all laughed, but Janeia knew better. She shook her
head and grinned nervously as she walked inside the hotel
lobby.

As soon as Molasses was out of earshot and inside the
hotel with his date, the first valet quizzed his fellow
employees.

"Who the hell was that?"

The second valet answered, "He's probably a ballplayer.
Maybe he's new with the Bears. He looks like a wide re-
ceiver or something. You know, like a flashy Keyshawn
Johnson type."

The first valet climbed into the car.

"Well, I hope he tips well," he hinted with a smile.

At the hotel check-in desk, Molasses stepped up with
Janeia at his side.

"May I help you?" a young Asian woman asked him. She
wore the black-and-white formal attire that was the uniform of the hotel's workers.

Molasses asked her, "I made reservations earlier for one
of your penthouse suites?"

The Asian woman raised a brow. The penthouse suites
were not normal money.

"Name?" she asked him.

"Warren Hamilton."

She worked her computer to find his reservation. "Ah,
yes. We have the Beverly Suite available for you."

She looked at Molasses again and said, "That'll be . . ."

Molasses cut her off with a raised hand.

"I know," he told her. He didn't need to hear the price again. He could afford the shit. Otherwise he wouldn't have asked for the room.

A young black male employee overheard the Beverly Suite and decided to comment on it.

"The Beverly Suite is nice, man. I wish I could afford to stay in there a few nights," he offered. "I feel rich just walking in there."

Everyone chuckled at it but Molasses. He eyed the man sternly instead.

He said, "That's great, but did I ask for your opinion on the room? Sometimes we have to learn how to mind our own business, *brother.*"

The black hotel employee got Molasses's message while reading the man's icy glare. He obviously wasn't to be fucked with. So the employee walked away without another word.

Janeia received their room key and followed Molasses to the elevators. When one arrived, they stepped in and regained their privacy.

Janeia immediately asked her man, "What was that all about?" She was puzzled by the outburst. What had the man done that was so wrong?

Molasses told her, "I don't trust big-mouth people. That's one of the first rules that you learn growing up in the 'hood. It's people like him who would be the first ones to talk."

He imitated a girlish voice to give his example, " 'Yes, sir, Mr. Officer. He did that, and he said this. And I *watched* him do it myself. Oh, yes, I'll testify in court.'

"Bitch-ass nigga!" Molasses concluded.

Janeia smiled at it.

"You are just too much," she told him.

"But that's why you like me, right?" he responded on cue. "Because if I was too *little*, I figure that a woman like you wouldn't give me the time of day."

Janeia sighed and felt guilty about it. She did enjoy the excesses of a man.

"I'm trying my best to work on that," she admitted.

They arrived on the twenty-fourth floor, the penthouse level, and walked into an awesome hotel suite. Deep, rich colors furnished the room, with a bottle of wine on ice at an elegant, two-seat dinner table.

Janeia looked and smiled. She was more than flattered by Molasses's romantic gestures.

"I see you went all out for this," she told him.

He only grinned at her.

He said, "If you can afford it, then why not indulge in some of life's luxuries?"

Janeia perused the spacious, well-decorated, multiroom suite and couldn't believe she was there.

"Oh, my God!" she expressed out loud.

Molasses went ahead and teased her about her excitement.

"Wait a minute, you're supposed to be working on that, right? You're supposed to be satisfied with anything? Just me, you, and the world."

Janeia laughed it off.

"Well, I'll work on it tomorrow," she told him.

They walked toward the penthouse deck together as the moonlight began to shine in the approaching darkness.

They stepped onto the large outside deck and enjoyed the Chicago breeze more than twenty stories up. They had been well fed at a restaurant earlier, and they were now expecting their dessert from each other, a blending of deep chocolate and creamed coffee.

Molasses made the first move as Janeia began to dream up a black Lois Lane and Superman scene.

"Come here. Let me feel your heart beat," he told her.

Janeia grinned and walked over to him.

Molasses spun her around and held her from behind. She folded her hands over his arms, and they stared up into the night together, overlooking the Chicago skyline.

"The sky looks beautiful, doesn't it?" Molasses asked her. Even a killer knew what was beautiful when he saw it.

He said, "You can see it so clearly from up here. It's like you can just reach out and touch it, and grab a piece of the moon."

Janeia smiled hard at that one.

She said, "You know what I figured out about you?"

Molasses was skeptical. He didn't like anyone trying to figure him out. He gave you what he wanted you to know and nothing more. Things were best that way.

"What's that?" he asked her.

Janeia said, "You got some strong-ass game."

Molasses grinned hard and felt guilty. She had him cornered with the truth.

He asked her, "Is that right?"

"Mmm, hmm. You know it, too. That's what's so dangerous about it," she told him.

"Well, you know what I figured out about you?" he asked her back.

It was Janeia's turn to grin.

"What's that?"

He said, "You can't help but be hip to the game. That's just who you are."

He spun Janeia back around to face him.

He told her right up close and in her pretty-ass face, "You can't turn it off, girl. You crafty. Marilyn Monroe.

Madonna. Diana Ross. You want that shit. The glamorous
life. And you can't even fake it."

Janeia looked into his eyes and found herself burning up
for him. His words struck her so deeply that she felt naked
and moist between the legs already. So she leaned into him
and kissed him hard on his lips.

Molasses returned her passion on the outside deck,
under a full moon as the stars began to appear. Piece by
piece, they pushed and pulled at each other's clothes until
they were both naked.

Molasses heaved Janeia's ready body into the air above
him. She then positioned him just right to enter her, and they
enjoyed a blissful ride under the moonlight, with their bodies
rowing up and down, in and out, and fast and slow toward
their shared and urgent satisfactions. She was giving him
every inch of her, and he was giving her every inch of him.

As the clock struck midnight, Molasses and Janeia were
naked and cuddled up under the warm sheets of the king-
size bed. They were both recuperating from the spent
energy of their ravenous heat.

Out of the blue Molasses told her, "I guess this is a
wrong time to ask you this. But are you on the pill or anything?"

Janeia smiled, wondering how much she could toy with
him or if he would allow her to toy at all.

"Would you kill me if I wasn't?" she asked him slyly. She
figured she was now close enough to him to spill at least a
sip of humor.

Molasses laughed and stopped.

He answered, "Maybe . . . maybe not."

Janeia paused.

"You told me you wouldn't kill a woman," she reminded
him.

"That's in business," he told her. "But this is *personal*. And you can ask O.J., the personal fucks up your mind more. You start doing shit you had no idea you would do."

Janeia read his cool-as-the-night demeanor and nodded to him.

"I'm on it," she answered. He was still able to scare the hell out of her. After all, he was a killer. He wasn't rapping about it and selling albums, he was actually doing the shit and getting paid well for it. She had no idea what he was really capable of.

Molasses said, "Good." And he spoke no more about it.

Janeia took a deep breath and climbed on top of him. Fuck it! She decided to go for broke and ride the devil through hell. If he could scare her that much, she figured it was well worth the ride.

She asked him, "How did you get the name Molasses, anyway?"

Molasses looked up at her and smiled.

He said, "An old lady who used to live in my building on the West Side would send me to the store for her. And every time I went, I would see my boys on the way and forget about it. So when I remembered and brought her her stuff back, she said . . ."

He stopped to imitate her raspy voice, " 'Boy, you sure are *sweet* compared to these other mean-ass kids around here. But you slow as *molasses* in gettin' ma food.' "

Janeia chuckled, imagining the whole scene.

"And that's how you got it?" she asked him.

"Wait a minute," he told her. "Don't cut me off. Learn to be a little more patient."

She grinned and pecked him on the lips.

Molasses continued with his story:

"Anyway, she was the only one who called me that until she saw me out the window one day and needed me to go to the store for her again. So she leans out the window and yells, 'Molasses! I need you to go to the store for me, boy!' And I'm thinking, *Aww, shit!* And that was it. Every day after that, 'Molasses this, Molasses that.' And I started beating people down for it. 'My name ain't Molasses.' But you know how niggas are."

He stopped and imitated the little black boys from his neighborhood, " 'Aw'ight, man, we won't call you that no more . . . *Molasses.*'

"So, you know, after a while I just got tired of bruising my damn knuckles over that name. And it stuck," he told her.

Janeia was enjoying every second of his company. She was all up in his face.

She took another breath and said, "I'm really diggin' you. I feel you all the way. And um . . . I'm not gon' pressure you. Or sweat you. It's just all about how I feel right now . . . and how I feel whenever I'm with you.

"I mean, I accept who you are and what you have to do out there. And I just want you to know that I'm here for you."

She spoke it to him with the purest dedication.

Molasses nodded to her.

He said, "That's good. That's exactly what I want. That's what I need. I just want you to *feel* for me."

Janeia thought about everything. And she agreed.

She said, "And if I feel for you like that . . . like I *do*. I just ask you to do one thing for me."

Molasses paused. He wasn't the one for making promises.

"And what's that?" he asked her. But just because he was asking didn't mean he was going to agree to the shit, no matter how much she dug him.

Janeia leaned her head into his left shoulder as she answered him.

"Don't ever leave me."

Molasses heard her loud and clear and chuckled at it. The chick had just lost her damn mind. But he decided to humor her anyway.

He said, "You know what? You got some strong-ass game."

Janeia smiled into his chest while they continued to rest up in bed and hold each other in the penthouse suite.

Needless to say, I was falling for him . . .
fast. And that's when you start
to ignore the obvious.

Back at Chicago State University, Janeia walked her girl Brenda toward her next class. They were both carrying bags filled with their books.

Janeia grinned and shook her head, still thinking about Molasses.

"What's that for?" Brenda asked her.

Janeia couldn't help herself.

"Girl, I am in so much trouble," she answered.

Brenda immediately looked concerned.

"With who? What did you do now?" she asked her love-struck and reckless friend. Life was not worth living to Janeia unless some new forbidden fruit was being tasted. And that was a dangerous-ass way to live.

Janeia answered, "I'm talking about with this new guy I'm seeing. I'm really feeling him."

Brenda frowned.

"Oh, as if that's never happened before."

"It's different now."

"How so?"

Janeia thought about it.

"Well, you know how I can usually bluff a guy?" She

stopped and shook her head before she continued. "That shit don't work with him. . . . And I like that."

Brenda stopped walking.

"You are out of your damn mind," she snapped. "You love yourself a damn head game. Something is really wrong with you. You must have a chemical imbalance or something."

Janeia kept on walking.

"Whatever."

Brenda stood there for a moment, just long enough to shake her head in disgust before she sped up to catch her girl.

DOWNTOWN at a tall Chicago office building, Molasses was making an afternoon visit to a female friend inside her office on the seventeenth floor. The blinds were closed to block out the views from the window. They didn't want any peeping Toms watching from the neighboring buildings.

"*Mmmph . . . mmmph . . . mmmph,*" the young businesswoman moaned as quietly as she could atop her desk.

Molasses was pushing and pulling between her legs as he stood at the edge of the desk, his pants down and his shirt hanging.

The young businesswoman had her dark gray skirt hiked up to her stomach, with her stockings and panties off. She was having herself a sneaky afternoon sexcapade.

"*Ooh shit . . . God,*" she whispered into Molasses's ear.

Molasses smiled into her face from his position over her.

"God can't help you right now," he teased her.

She laughed quietly.

"Ssshhh, stop it," she told him.

"Stop what? *This?*" Molasses asked her with a sudden thrust of his hips.

She became squeamish.

"No, not that," she moaned.

Outside of her office, there was a busy workday going on with plenty of company employees doing their jobs.

However, back inside the young woman's private office, Molasses was driving her toward a strong climax. He began to thrust faster and harder, finding himself approaching a strong one himself.

"Damn, you got some good shit," he whispered to her. "Does your husband think so?"

She was now incoherent, engrossed in the excitement of the moment.

"Huh? Ooh, ooh."

On her windowsill was a picture of her family of four, with two young daughters. Everyone was smiling. But back on her desk, where the family pictures normally sat, an adulterous climax was being reached.

The young businesswoman grabbed on tightly and locked her legs around Molasses's ass as he jerked into her and tightened his face in bliss with hers.

And when they had finished, they *both* exhaled.

"Shit! I'm gon' have to make you a regular lunch break," Molasses told her.

She chuckled and reminded him that they were still under time constraints at her office. So they struggled up and began to re-dress. She then sprayed her office with the air freshener from her bottom desk drawer.

"That was *great*," she told her mischievous friend.

Molasses took the paper towels that she had given him and pulled off a soiled condom to discard. She took it from him and tossed it in a plastic Ziploc bag.

Molasses grabbed his briefcase from the floor and slid his sports jacket back on. The young office chick straightened out her clothes, made sure her hair was in order in the van-

ity mirror from her purse, and reopened her blinds before
they prepared to walk back out of the office together.

She smiled at Molasses right before she opened the
office door.

"Call me," she told him.

Molasses smiled back.

"You know I will."

They kissed one last time before opening the door and
walking out in good, friendly spirits.

The other employees were all eyes as soon as they
walked out of the office. Particularly the women—black,
white, Latin, *and* Asian.

"Oh, and tell Parker I said hi," Molasses bullshitted to
his hot married friend in reference to her sucker of a husband.

"I sure will," she responded to him with a glow.

A few of the women looked on and knew better. Even
some of the guys were assuming things. They just didn't
have any proof.

So Molasses winked at a cute brown secretary and continued on his way to the elevators, undiscovered.

The secretary was intrigued by the man. But after his
wink, she immediately looked back at her boss to catch her
response to it.

The young businesswoman frowned at her with the
intimidation factor of authority. The secretary then
dropped her head and got back to work, realizing that her
married boss had a thing for the attractive "friend" herself.

INSIDE the parking garage at the lower levels of the building, Molasses climbed into his Bentley, selected his music,
and drove off.

He cruised comfortably through the downtown streets of
Chicago, checking out all the folks who checked him out,

particularly the multitudes of curious women. Molasses loved their attention. He couldn't get enough of them. So instead of being a hit man who hid in the dark, he enjoyed the spoils of his dark life while out in the light.

He entered a Wendy's drive-thru for a Frosty and made a call from his car phone while waiting his turn to order. He sat behind two cars and put his caller on the speaker system.

The sexy voice of a woman answered.

"Hello."

Molasses smiled at her tempting tone.

"Damn, you make it sound like you knew I was calling."

The woman laughed.

"Don't flatter yourself," she told him. Then she stopped. "Wait a minute, do you have me on that car phone thing again?"

Molasses continued to smile from the cabin of his plush ride.

"What can I say? I love hearing the sound of your voice in stereo," he told her.

"Do you love *seeing* me?" she asked him.

Molasses stopped smiling.

He answered, "Yeah, that, too." But he didn't really mean the shit. Certain women did different things for his ego, and he mainly liked the sound of her voice, and her strong blow jobs.

"So when can you see me again?" she pressed him.

"Soon. I just don't know how soon."

She let out a deep sigh over the phone, amplified by his stereo system.

"You have that many house calls to make, huh?" she assumed.

Molasses moved his car up in the drive-thru line. He smiled again, anticipating her reaction to his response.

"Don't make me brag about it," he told her.

She heard that and said, "Oh, shit. That's so foul. You are just . . ."

Molasses cut her off before she could finish.

He said, "I'll call you back in a few," and he hung up on her without even a good-bye.

He moved up to the menu and speaker board at Wendy's just so the cashier could flood his ears with her bad-day nastiness.

"Can I take your order?" she asked in a monotone. Her voice spoke volumes about what she felt of her job.

Molasses took in her tone and frowned into the speaker.

"Damn! What's all that about?"

"Look, can I take your order, please?"

Molasses shook his head.

He said, "All I want is a Frosty."

"What size?"

"Medium."

"Your total is one seventy-nine. Pay at the first window."

"Yeah, thank you very much," he told the woman.

He drove up to the first window and took out a twenty-dollar bill. He looked up into the cashier's booth and eyed an overstressed black woman in her late twenties with a case of bad skin.

He offered her the twenty-dollar bill.

"You need love in your life that you're not gettin', don't you?" he asked.

The stress-filled woman looked at his handsome brown face, his nice clothes, and his Bentley, and her coldhearted demeanor melted into a warm smile.

She took his payment and commented to him boldly, "Why don't *you* give me some?"

Molasses responded with a straight face.

"Sorry, I'm not the man for that job. But I'll tell you what, I'll let you keep that change so you can work on changing your attitude. Okay?" He drove off to the second window for his Frosty before the cashier could respond to him.

She sucked her teeth when he left and mumbled, "Motherfucker." But she sure pocketed that money, and went right back to her job.

"Can I take your order?"

BACK on the busy streets of Chicago, Molasses continued to cruise in his Bentley while drinking his Frosty from Wendy's. He drove right past a Chicago police cruiser and paid it no mind. They didn't have shit on him.

Inside the police cruiser was the same black cop who had spotted Molasses in his Bentley just a few days ago when he picked up Janeia on the South Side. Officer Barrett was on his private cell phone again.

"Yeah, man, I think I'm gonna look into a detective position. I'm even considering working for the FBI nowadays," he was telling one of his friends on the Chicago police force.

He spotted Molasses cruising by in his Bentley.

Molasses, unaware that the black cop was still watching him from his police cruiser, tossed his trash out of the window as he drove down the next block. Who the hell wants to keep trash inside a Bentley?

However, littering on public property was not a good thing to do, particularly when a cop was itching for a reason to question you.

Officer Barrett began to smile from behind his wheel.

"Let me call you back," he told his friend on the other end of his phone call.

He hung up the cell phone and flicked on his siren to run Molasses down and pull him over.

Whurrp! Whurrp! Whurrp!

Inside his Bentley, Molasses heard the police siren and looked into his rearview mirror.

"I know this asshole ain't after me," he grumbled to himself. Nevertheless, the police cruiser pulled up right behind him. So who the hell else would he be after?

Molasses pulled his Bentley over and stopped at the curb in the middle of the busy Chicago street. The police cruiser pulled up behind him with the lights still flashing and plenty of passersby looking on.

Officer Barrett stepped out of his police cruiser in his dark blue uniform, with badges, a nightstick, his gun, and a ticket pad and pen in hand. He walked up to the driver's-side window and waited for Molasses to roll it down.

Molasses slowly pressed down his window.

"Can I help you with anything, Officer?"

Officer Barrett responded to him sternly.

"Do you understand that street littering is a seventy-five-dollar fine?"

Molasses snapped his fingers. "My bad, brother. It just slipped my mind. You know, when you own a car like this one, you don't want to carry any trash around in it."

The officer ignored his boast and moved on with his official business.

"May I see your license, registration, and insurance, please?"

Molasses became skeptical.

"You don't think I stole this car, do you?"

Officer Barrett answered him snidely.

"Oh, not at all. You know, when a young man drives around in a car like *this one*, I just *assume* that he can afford it."

Molasses smiled at the cop's return volley of sarcasm. He then dug up all of his information and handed it over. The officer took it and checked everything out at his squad car. He then wrote out a ticket.

A black man looking on from the sidewalk strolled up

and shook his head during the process. He was the black militant type, disgusted by all the continued police harassment of black men in America. He especially didn't like that a *black* officer was harassing a brother in broad daylight.

He said, "It's a shame a black man can't drive a nice car like that without being pulled over. It's called D-W-B."

Officer Barrett ignored the man and finished his business. He handed Molasses back his information, along with the ticket for littering. He then stood there at the window for a minute.

"So, what kind of work do you do?" he asked Molasses.

Molasses told him, "I do security for young entertainers and athletes."

Then he smiled, and added, "You know, they have plenty of money nowadays and people are pretty good for sweatin' them for their time. In fact, I kind of feel like one of them right now."

The officer nodded as if he believed him.

"Who are some of the people you've worked with?" he asked.

"Are you ready to hire me for a job?" Molasses asked him, dodging an answer.

"Maybe," Officer Barrett humored him.

Molasses nodded to him.

"Well, that information is confidential."

"Do you have a business card?" the officer asked him next.

Molasses pulled out a platinum card holder from his sports jacket and opened it up to hand the cop one of his business cards.

The card read "PRIME TIME SECURITY, *Keeping the stars safe and sound,*" with contact information below.

The officer nodded and said, "I'll be giving you a call . . . *Warren.*"

Molasses looked him over and responded snidely.

"Look, I don't do much charity work anymore. I mean, I started off that way, man, but you know, that thing called inflation . . ." He shook his head. "It just kills you," he added.

The officer stared at him a minute.

He grinned and said, "I see. Inflation is just beating you to death."

Molasses smiled and restarted his engine.

"Thanks for your time, Officer."

The black cop took a lingering stare as the Bentley drove off down the street. He then walked back to his squad car to resume his cell phone call.

"Hey, man, how much do you know about the celebrity security business?"

THAT night at The Lake, one of Chicago's finer and more expensive restaurants, Molasses spent quality time wining and dining Janeia Goode for another night on the town. They were both dressed to impress sitting at a fine mahogany dinner table, enjoying a tall bottle of dark wine from skinny glasses with gold trim. To their left, they shared a perfect view of Lake Michigan through a fourteen-foot window.

Janeia was still smiling at Molasses's story of the day.

She said, "I would imagine that you would get pulled over a lot in that car. I heard that Bentleys cost a lot of money."

He said, "They do. They cost more than I would pay for."

He took a sip of his drink.

Janeia looked surprised by his comment.

She asked him, "You didn't pay for it?"

Molasses frowned at her with his drink still in hand.

He said, "Hell no! I drove a Navigator. It cost me *a fourth* of the price of this Bentley."

Janeia smiled and waited for him to explain while she sipped her drink. How did he receive the car in the first place? She knew he had a story about it. Molasses had a story for everything.

He said, "I had an, uh, *employer* who suffered from rule number two: pay me my money. So when he came up short, I had to charge him interest."

"That's a whole lot of interest," she commented.

"Yeah, well, it was either the car or his life," Molasses told her.

She shook her head and grinned.

Molasses stood from the table.

"I gotta make a fast run to the restroom. Make sure you don't get lost on me."

"I'm sure you'll find me if I do," she joked.

Molasses left her for the men's restroom.

On the other side of the restaurant, a deep-brown black woman in a black-and-gold dress watched them from her table. She was one of Molasses's old flings. When she saw him heading for the restrooms, she stood up and excused herself from her own date to intercept Molasses on his return.

As soon as Molasses finished his business inside the bathroom, he was caught off guard on the way back to his table.

"Hi, stranger," his old fling told him with a sly smile.

Molasses was hesitant to engage in a conversation with her. Pamela Riggs was one of his more dramatic choices, a privileged chick with a little bit of money. She had been spoiled by far too many jelly-spined men long before he had ever met her. He now considered her a big mistake, so he chose to keep a safe distance from her, and out of her pompous life.

"Hi," he responded to her. It was all he planned to say.

She said, "Can I ask you a question?"

"Make it a quick one," he told her.

"Why you disappear on me, Moe? What did I do wrong? I mean, I stayed loyal to you."

Molasses told her sternly, "Look, Pam, this is not the time nor the place for this. Okay?"

Pam immediately became indignant.

"Well, when is it then? *Obviously*, you don't know how to *call* me anymore."

Molasses even tried to whisper to her.

"Girl, don't you fuck with me. You hear me? Now go on back to what you were doing before you get more than your feelings hurt."

Pam gave him a hard, pained stare before she turned to walk away. She spoke not another word. She knew Molasses meant what he said. She had witnessed his anger, and it was ferocious. So she tactfully got to stepping.

Back at their table, Janeia watched the tail end of the nasty exchange between Molasses and his old plaything, and knew. Women could just tell when shit was foul. They had radar for it.

Janeia only hesitated for a second before she asked Molasses about it.

"What was that about?"

Molasses shook his head and was still irritated by it. His night had been going perfectly.

He said, "Some people just can't handle when it's over."

Janeia looked into his eyes at that moment and read his coldness. How long would it be before her time was up?

She dropped her eyes away from him right as the food arrived at their table. The waiter set down their exquisite steak dinners.

Molasses took a strong whiff of the food and forced himself to cheer up. He refused to let some old chick fuck up his night with his new one.

He said excitedly, "All right! Time to get down to business!"

Janeia barely smiled and said nothing. She looked saddened. However, Molasses paid her no mind. He began to cut into his food with both hands. Janeia picked into her food slowly. She had lost her appetite. All she could think about was Molasses leaving her. How long did she really expect to be able to keep him?

She knew the game. The real thug niggas were the hardest to keep. The only balls and chains that seemed heavy enough to lock them down were prison . . . and the graveyard.

The oldest saying in the book is "Momma knows best." . . . But how many of us really bother to listen to her?

On a sunny afternoon on the South Side, Janeia rode a public bus back home from school, watching high school couples enjoying each other's company, smiling and holding hands. Jancia eyed them and cracked a smile herself, thinking about her man, Molasses. She was dressed brightly and colorfully to cheer herself up for the day, including a new hairstyle that fell past her shoulders.

She climbed down from the bus once she reached the edge of the block of 83rd Street, where she lived with her mother. She walked up the block of redbrick, single-family homes and pulled out a key as she approached their walkway. She hustled up the gray cement steps, opened the white screen, and unlocked the light brown wooden door. She then entered her home of the past twelve years.

There was nothing eye-popping or fancy about where she lived. Besides the normal furniture that any house would have, there were photos of various relatives during various years, along with framed artwork that hung in the larger open spaces of the eggshell-colored walls.

"Mom!" Janeia yelled in no particular direction.

The tired voice of her overworked mother sounded off from the kitchen area toward the back of the house.

"I'm in here, girl."

Janeia tossed her bag of school things on the living room sofa and strolled into the kitchen. She found her mother eating a bowl of Cheerios with milk. She was dressed in only her housecoat and slippers.

Janeia looked her mother over and shook her head with a grin. The woman was barely forty, but she carried herself as if she had lived twice as long.

"What?" she asked her daughter. She knew Janeia was smiling at something. She then considered her clothes and the bowl of cereal at midday.

"Oh, girl, I don't have to dress up on my off days. That's the difference between me and you. Your behind will find a way to dress up for the damn mailman," she commented. "Spending all that good grant money on clothes and hairstyles. You'll learn soon enough."

Janeia took a seat across from her at their small oval-shaped table that sat to the right side of the kitchen.

"I'm still using the grant for my education," she stated in her own defense.

"Yeah, because you *have* to. You need to think more about completing your education than impressing these feebleminded young guys out here, I'll tell you that much," her mother advised her.

She said, "You think I haven't noticed how you've just been floatin' around this house lately, and goin' out for nights at a time?"

Janeia had not gone straight to college out of high school. She had waited a few years, still undecided about her future. And her dealings with fast men had a lot to do with her indecisiveness.

"Mom, stop," she piped.

"Well, just tell me this. How come I don't get to meet any of them anymore?" her mother asked her.

Janeia sighed and looked away. As far as she was concerned, her personal business was hers alone, unless she had
invited her mother into it, which she had not done of late.

"Because it's not really serious like that," she answered.

Her mother waited to read her eyes before she commented
further on it. But Janeia refused to look at her. So she gave up
on the eye contact and frowned at her daughter instead.

She said, "Girl, pack up that bullshit and take it out of
the house somewhere. You've been more brokenhearted
than me and all of your aunts put together, and you only
half our age. And then you gon' sit up in here and tell me
you ain't *serious,*" she mocked her.

"You must think I'm a damn *fool,*" her mother continued
to snap. "You're *too* serious about these damn *frivolous* guys.
That's what your problem is. And you keep choosing the
wrong damn ones."

Janeia took it all in and thought about her long-gone
father and the countless men who had marched in and out
of her mother's life.

She mumbled, "Well, it ain't like I learned anything
good from you."

Her mother was caught off guard by it. But what the
hell, the shit was true. Mother and daughter were both
drama queens. By the time her mother opened her mouth
to respond, the front doorbell rang and interrupted them.

They looked at each other momentarily and wondered
who would go and answer it. But it was still Mom's house,
and she still wielded the frying pan and paid the mortgage.
So she surely didn't expect to lose that discussion.

She said, "I hope you don't think that *I'm* gettin' that,"
and went back to eating her cereal.

"It ain't for me anyway," she assumed.

Janeia grinned and stood back up from the kitchen table
to answer the front door.

Outside in the doorway was Rasheed, a neighborhood good guy with his own style of dress and social beliefs. He was a light-brown brother wearing tailor-made cotton clothes with a matching bucket hat. He was a throwback to the black power era of the urban sixties and seventies, when black folks tried to uplift themselves through education, politics, and American integration. But who cared about that shit in the new millennium. The 'hood had now reverted back to the days of the forties and fifties, when segregated thug niggas pimped and conned each other. The new-wave niggas were all about the street life now, and the masses were proudly following their self-destructive lead.

Nevertheless, die-hard do-gooders like Rasheed continued to carry a semblance of hope to reverse the regressive plight of the masses. So he waited patiently at Janeia's door and snapped his fingers to a jazzy beat in his head.

Janeia answered the door and eyed Rasheed skeptically. What the hell did he want? She hadn't spoken to his square ass in years. She played it off and grinned at him anyway, as if she was happy to see his do-good ass.

Rasheed extended his arms to her like a welcoming committee.

"Happy to see me back?" he asked her.

Janeia went along with the shit and hugged him. But when she did, she disengaged quicker than he expected and left him hanging for more. That's what the squares did, they hung on to thin air, hoping and praying for good things to happen for them.

Rasheed even joked to massage his damaged ego.

"I guess you're only happy to see me a little bit."

Janeia ignored it.

"So, how's the music business going?" she asked him.

She at least remembered what the boy was into the last time she saw him. He was one of those old-school, hip-hop fanatics, steady starving to get signed to a recording contract.

Rasheed frowned at her when he responded.

He said, "You ain't heard none of my songs? You don't have the album?"

Janeia smiled and nodded, still faking the game.

"Yeah, I've heard them." But she still didn't give a fuck. Good for him, he finally had a record deal and a couple of singles out. She never bought his album though. She wasn't turned on by his kind of music. It wasn't really . . . *hard* enough. So she could just imagine what his sex was like. *Soft*, just like his music. So she avoided all of his advances.

Rasheed went on to brag about his success anyway.

He said, "Come on now, I know you heard my music. Don't front on me like that. The home spot gotta show me some love!"

Janeia grinned and decided to help him out in his boasting.

She said, "I guess you got a lot of groupies and stuff sweatin' you now, huh?"

He answered, "Nah, I don't need all of that. I just want one special girl to sweat me. And I want to sweat her right back."

He stopped and started rapping to her, *"And we can sweat each other together in love / while we take warm showers to make it better in bad weather. Yeah, that's the kind of girl I wanna sweat wit' / Mary J. Blige said I need real love like Black Panther leather / so I never sport that fake, plastic shit."*

Janeia smiled at him, impressed with his confident delivery. He didn't miss a beat.

She said, "Okay, okay, I'm sure that my mom would like to see you," and opened the door wide to invite him in.

Rasheed grinned and said, "Yeah, let me holla' at her."

They walked inside the house and headed back toward the kitchen.

"Who is it, Janeia?" her mother asked before they arrived.

Janeia gave Rasheed a finger to her lips for silence. When they arrived at the kitchen, she said, "Hey, Mom, look what the cat brought in."

Her mother spotted the neighborhood good boy and was excited as hell. Rasheed was a sight for sore eyes, looking tall, healthy, handsome, and *good*!

She even stood up from her chair to give him a stronger hug than her daughter had.

"Rasheed! Hi you doin', boy?"

She stepped back and gave him another look.

"Boy, you lookin' good and smellin' good and everything! Are you married yet?" she hinted.

Rasheed laughed it off.

"Nah, not yet, Ms. Goode. I'm still young. I'm looking, though. But I need me a down-home sister. You know, a sister who know the struggle."

Janeia's mom joked with him.

"Oh, yeah, well, have you met my daughter, Janeia? She's been struggling. But I can work on her for you if you need me to."

Janeia said, "I think you've done enough of that already, Mom."

"No, I haven't. Not *even*," her mother begged to differ. "You need plenty of work to come on back down to reality. She still like them damn rough types, thinkin' they gon' *mature* one day."

Rasheed nodded. He was in agreement with Mom.

He said, "I know. That's the hot thing to be now, a black villain. And you 'sposed to be proud of it, too."

Janeia said, "Yeah, whatever. I guess I'll just leave you two alone to talk then," and she walked out of the kitchen.

Her mother immediately shook her head at her daughter's antics.

She then whispered to Rasheed, "I don't know what's wrong with that girl sometimes."

"She'll be aw'ight, Ms. Goode. Sometimes we just need time," he advised.

"Ain't it the damn truth," she responded to him. "So, how have things been going for you?"

Rasheed was proud to talk about it.

He said, "Oh, everything is going real well for me. I can't complain too much. I've been around the world now.

"You gotta get out there just to expand your horizons," he told her. "World travel is a good thing to do for a black man, to get him away from that one depiction of himself."

Janeia's mother shook her head with a proud smile that stretched across her face.

She said, "And I know your mother's proud."

"Oh, no doubt, no doubt," Rasheed confirmed. "She real proud."

BACK at the front of the house, Janeia escorted Rasheed out the door to conclude his surprise visit.

He stopped her on the cement steps and asked her, "So, what's up, Janeia? When we gon' go out again and talk about new things? Just me and you?"

Janeia shook her head and tried to turn him down easy.

"I mean, I always thought you were cute, Rasheed, but . . ."

She just wasn't feeling his ass on the real gusto level. He didn't have what she needed. She was bored with that boy just in talking to him. She was more familiar with stress and friction in life, and Rasheed gave her none of it. His peace of mind was alien to her.

He cut her off anyway and was desperate to plead his case.

He said, "*Cute?* Girl, I'm a grown man now. That ain't

how you describe a grown-ass man. Shit, can I at least get a *handsome*?"

Janeia smiled and nodded to him.

"Yeah, I'll give you that. You're handsome."

"But no date?" he pressed her.

Janeia just stared at him with pity in her eyes.

She mumbled to him as if she was ashamed to say it.

"No."

Rasheed stood there and paused.

He said, "All right then, Janeia. I guess you'll just keep breaking my heart. And I'ma write a song about you, too."

"Just don't use my name," she told him.

Rasheed was disappointed to hear that. He thought they were cool.

He said, "Damn! That's some cold-blooded shit."

But so what? She had her life . . . and he had his.

Rasheed walked away to a white Lexus SUV that was parked at the curb. He looked back, but Janeia had already slipped back inside.

Rasheed climbed into his comfortable Lexus, clicked on his music, and drove off.

Back inside the house, Janeia's mother stepped away from the window where she had watched her daughter give Rasheed the cold shoulder. She frowned as soon as she met eyes with her daughter.

She said, "You know what, girl? Rasheed has a lot of good, common sense in him. I just wish *you* had some sometimes.

"And you know what else?" she added. "You can sit in here and talk about my life all you want, but when you make the same mistakes, then it's all about *your* life. So don't blame me for shit."

Janeia ignored her. It *was* her life, and she had a right to share it with whomever she chose to. Rasheed just wasn't her choice of a partner.

So I had to learn the hard way. For Molasses, everything came down to business as usual.

That same sunny afternoon on a deserted street near Chicago's midtown, Molasses was parked in his black Navigator with Charlie, his business partner in the hit-man racket. They had been doing business now for three years, and Molasses had learned to trust Charlie's precision, cool head, and loyalty more than he trusted anyone. He was skeptical of the underground-connected white boy on the first few jobs, but after that, they began to deal with the business of killing on a level of calculated science.

Charlie had a way of finding desperate folks with real money to pay for jobs well done. Molasses found that working with him was a big come-up from the low-life street kills. And Charlie found that Molasses was one of the smoothest killers that he could ever work with. So their business together became lovely.

Inside the high-seated Navigator, Molasses looked over Charlie's computer printouts. They were photos and details for new contracts.

Molasses stopped at a picture of a brown-haired white woman and held it in his lap.

"Hey, man, I'm not too good at judging white girls. Would you fuck her?" he asked Charlie.

They never used each other's real names.

Molasses showed Charlie the photo to give him another good look. The girl had model and movie star potential.

Charlie looked at the brown-haired beauty and smiled. She looked hot enough for him.

He nodded and said, "Definitely. In all kinds of ways."

Molasses grinned and nodded back to him.

He said, "Yeah, me too. I was just fucking with you. I know a bad bitch when I see one. I don't care what race she is. She could be a motherfuckin' Martian, but if she fine, she fine. And this white girl right here is doing it for me."

Charlie laughed and stroked the new hairs of his fresh goatee. He wasn't a bad-looking white boy himself. He had that urban-white-boy look, the ones who could hang out in the 'hood and score with a few black chicks. Shit, Charlie had a few bling-bling dreams of his own. That's why he treasured dealing with Molasses. The black man could bring him some real cheese, though sometimes he could go a little overboard with his ego and exotic tastes. He lived a little too flashy now for a sensible hit man. He had to be reminded that they were in a criminal racket.

Charlie said, "I've been meaning to tell you this, Moe, but I think you need to stop mixing women with business, if you know what I mean. It's just a bad idea."

Molasses heard him and ignored him. He was still looking over the information on the white woman.

"So her husband wants us to knock off this guy here, to keep his wife from sleeping around?" he asked Charlie for clarity.

He looked over two more photos of white men. The first picture was a handsome, young white man with chiseled features. The second picture was a beer-bellied husband who looked more like a sit-on-his-ass-and-talk-shit-to-the-television sports fanatic.

Charlie nodded and said, "Yeah."

Molasses continued to view the printouts.

He finally said, "I hate to say it, man, but this ugly-ass husband of hers looks like he crawled up outta the swamp somewhere. He don't need to kill nobody to keep his wife. He needs a fuckin' *face-lift*! Goddamn plastic surgery or something!"

Charlie said, "He's offering a hundred thousand dollars."

"For what?" Molasses questioned. "So she can cry her eyes out and then go out and fuck the next guy. She'll probably do it right after the funeral."

Charlie chuckled a minute.

Molasses continued with his assessment of the job.

He shook his head and declined it.

"I ain't feeling this one, man. I'd keep this girl as one of my women," he leveled with his partner. "Then her ugly-ass husband would want to kill me. What else we got?" he asked, moving on. He tossed the photos back into Charlie's lap.

Charlie handed him other printouts. Molasses took them and looked them over.

The first photo was a sexy, young Latin woman. The second photo was a strong-bodied Latin man. He was older and looked like the enforcer type, a real bruiser.

"Okay, what's their story?" Molasses asked his partner.

Charlie answered, "She's a young singer from Miami. She claims that this guy forced his way into managing her. And she says that he's taking her to the cleaners on her advances and royalties. On top of that, he basically humps her whenever he wants to and fucks with her social life."

Molasses thought it over.

"So how come she just don't blow the whistle on him? *Star* magazine would love this story," he commented.

Charlie answered, "She's ashamed of it. And she wants to

keep her image intact. So she wants us to make it look like a
hit from underworld sources."

"What, he's in the Latin mafia down in Miami? Fuckin'
Scarface and his Cuban crew?" Molasses joked.

Charlie smiled. "Yeah, something like that," he answered.

"How much is it worth to her?"

Charlie smiled again.

"Two hundred fifty thousand dollars," he answered.

Molasses looked over at him to make sure.

"She got that kind of money?"

"She's worth *millions*," Charlie assured him.

Molasses said, "Well, shit, Charlie, this one is easy."

He nodded his head, pleased with it. He then looked
over at his eager partner and grinned.

He said, "You doin' pretty good for yourself in this business, Charlie. That Internet shit is amazing. Do you miss
working with them computer geeks?"

Charlie answered, "Not hardly. And ah . . . I was never a
geek," he added.

Molasses ignored him again. He looked at the photo of
the Latin manager and said, "I'll get this motherfucker for
sure."

He then joked about it while shaking the printout in
both his hands. "Leave her alone, *Sammy*! You big *bully*!"

Charlie laughed it off again. Molasses had a full personality, that was for sure. He wasn't just some dark, dangerous
grunt. He had a lot of character to him. Maybe too much.

Outside on the sidewalk a young black couple showed up
out of the blue and started yelling at each other. A young
thug, dressed in the latest hip-hop sports fashion, was all up
in his woman's face.

Charlie immediately put his things back in his black bag
inside the Navigator.

"So what happened to the rest of the fuckin' money, if

you made the deal?" the young thug pressed his woman. It was that kind of a street, an underground hideaway.

She said, "I told you. That's all that was in there."

The sweet, chocolate brown girl had a sassy flair of her own, wearing a high, black leather skirt and tall, black leather boots. She didn't look the innocent type at all. She had curves that told a story of their own.

The young thug continued to snap at her.

"So you let this motherfucker take you? You's a stupid-ass bitch! I *swear*!"

"Well, you should have did it your *damn self* then! Since *you* so fuckin' *smart*!" the sassy girl snapped back at him. "But no, you were trying to use *me* for that shit."

He then grabbed her by her neck and started to choke the life out of her.

"Bitch, who da fuck you think you talkin' to?"

Before Charlie knew it, Molasses had hopped out of the vehicle. He was on the case, like some kind of urban super-hero.

"Let her go, man," he told the young thug calmly.

The boy turned and spotted Molasses's nickel-plated nine-millimeter pointed right at his nose. He immediately let the sassy woman go.

"This ain't got nothing to do with you, man," he told Molasses.

"Now it does," Molasses responded to him.

He then smacked the young thug to the ground with his left hand. Charlie watched and slid down low inside the Navigator. He didn't want the extra attention.

The sassy woman remained still and calm with large eyes while Molasses did his hero thing.

The thug climbed back to his feet with anger in his eyes. What the fuck was this guy's problem?

The superhero asked him, "You ever heard of Molasses?"

The young thug blinked and felt his busted lip without speaking a word. Sure, he had heard of the whispered-about, Chicago street killer. So he nodded.

Molasses told him, "Well, now you just met him. So go ahead and run along before I practice my aim on your ass."

The ego-damaged boy looked at the black Navigator and kept his cool for a second. He then started to jog backward. When he finally turned to speed up his pace, he looked back every step of the way to make sure he didn't catch a bullet in the ass.

Molasses turned to the sassy, chocolate sister and took out a business card. He looked her right in her eyes to nail his intent in her head.

He said, "If you ever fantasize about feeling love from a real man, I want you to give me a call. All right?"

She took the card and stared back at him. She was definitely interested.

She said, "Okay. I'll do that."

Molasses walked back to his Navigator while the girl continued to eye him.

He looked back and said, "You call me. All right?"

She smiled at him.

"I will."

Back inside the Navigator, Molasses restarted his engine and drove off.

He looked over at his worrisome partner and said, "Charlie, did you see the *body* on that girl? My *God*! What are they *eating* nowadays?"

He stopped and added, "See now, they don't make white girls like that, Charlie. Y'all got them six o'clock women, straight up and straight down. Either that, or them three o'clock women with breast-implanted titties and no ass."

Charlie just shook his head.

He said, "That's exactly what I'm talking about, Moe. You can't keep mixing your sex life with our business."

Molasses looked at him again and frowned.

He said, "Oh, I get it. I'm supposed to be the black man in the movie, right? So I do all the running around and the dirty work, like some Jim Brown character, but with no pussy, while you go home and make love to your lovely wife.

"Yeah, well, fuck that shit, Charlie! That's that old-time religion," Molasses snapped at him. "But it's a new fuckin' day now. And what's the use in me having this life and all these women falling for me if I can't get down with them?"

He said, "You gotta be out of your damn mind, Charlie. So I'm gon' get all the pussy I can get. And you can *quote me* on that."

Charlie was still shaking his head.

He said, "All right? You just remember that I told you so. And by the way," he added with a grin, "I don't have a lovely wife yet."

Molasses chuckled and grinned back at him.

He said, "Not yet, but you'll find one . . . if you haven't found her already. You just keep fuckin' with me. You'll be able to buy the finest white bitch you want."

But since I had unconditional love for him, I just had to wait my turn.

On a new day at Chicago State University, Janeia walked with her girl Brenda toward the bus stop on campus. And Brenda was steady running her big mouth.

"Girl, Rasheed's album is definitely *banging*! And you know he gettin' paid now. I mean, what more could you want?"

Janeia spotted Dollar Bill heading in their direction. She looked at him and sighed.

"Not him, I'll tell you that," she commented to her friend.

Brenda spotted the part-time student/hustler and frowned herself. But that didn't deter him from speaking to them.

He said, "What's up, Janeia? You start thinking about *us* yet?"

"Whenever I have nightmares," she told him.

Brenda smiled at the line.

But Dollar Bill kept up the flow. He nodded to Janeia real cool and asked, "So, are your panties on or off when you're having these nightmares?"

The two girlfriends decided to ignore him and keep walking. They could see now that they weren't gonna win a dispute with him. The boy was a king at the mouth.

So even as they ignored him, he had something to say.

"I'm telling you, Janeia, you'll get the red carpet treatment with me. Aw'ight? I promise. And I don't make many promises."

As he continued to nag them and follow them toward the bus stop, Molasses pulled up in his Bentley at the curb.

He jumped right out and walked over toward the small-time hustler, who immediately stopped yapping his mouth and nodded to him. No words were needed. He knew who Molasses was.

Janeia stopped walking and smiled at her man.

"What a surprise! And it's not even my birthday," she joked to him.

She stepped up to hug Molasses, while Brenda and Dollar Bill looked on in silence. They were both at a loss for words. Janeia had really stepped up her game this time. The nigga drove a *Bentley*.

Molasses told her, "Let's go for a ride."

Janeia looked back to Brenda.

"I'll call you," she told her friend.

Brenda was still standing in suspended animation.

"Okay."

What else could she say? She was still shocked.

Janeia climbed into the Bentley with Molasses and drove off with him.

Dollar Bill was stunned by the experience himself.

He said, "Shit! Well, there goes *my* game."

Brenda still needed an explanation.

"So, you obviously know him. . . . Who is he?" she asked.

The hustler shook his head and declined to speak on it for once.

"You don't even wanna know. That motherfucka *crazy.* "

INSIDE the Bentley, Molasses looked over at Janeia in the passenger seat. He asked her, "So, how was your day?"

She shrugged. It was no big deal to her. It was just school.

"The same as usual," she answered. *"B-o-r-i-n-g."*

"And what about now?" he teased her.

She grinned at him.

"And now it's exciting . . . and about to end with a bang," she hinted.

Molasses smiled and thought for a beat.

"That was your girlfriend with you?" he asked her.

She answered, "Yeah."

"So, what did you tell her about us?"

He was curious. Girls talked constantly about their love life, especially to their main girlfriend.

But Janeia answered, "Not much. I mean, I told her that I feel for you a great deal, but she doesn't know much more than that. She doesn't even know your name."

Molasses nodded and was pleased to hear it. The girl didn't need to know his name.

He said, "Good. We need to keep it that way."

He looked at Janeia to nail his point.

"Everything we do stays right here between us. You hear me?"

She paused, and thought her own thoughts about it.

She said, "I know that already. But what about you driving up to my school, unannounced and whatnot? I mean, it was nice, but doesn't it bring us unwanted attention?"

She was right. Molasses was fucking up his own game.

He joked it off and said, "Shit, I'm not Batman. I can show up in the daytime. I just don't want people talking about me. You know? So I'm gonna be *seen* but *unseen.* 'Cause I don't live in no damn cave. What fun is that?"

Janeia thought about that for a minute, particularly his use of the word *fun.*

"So, this is all *fun* to you? That's what it's all about?" she asked him.

He looked at her and said, "What's it all about for you?"

Janeia paused again.

"Love," she answered.

Molasses stopped to look at her. She looked back and was dead serious. Molasses reached over and squeezed her hand in his. He had her wide open. He was really beginning to feel for this young chick.

THEY ended up taking an afternoon walk at the park on Lakeshore Drive along Lake Michigan. They held hands and the whole nine, like true romance.

Janeia looked out at the city-side view of the massive body of blue water and felt invincible. She felt as if the world was at her fingertips for a minute. She could go anywhere and do anything.

So she asked her man, "Have you ever been on a cruise?"

Molasses brought her back to earth when he answered.

He said, "Are you kidding me? I'm a black man. I'm afraid of the water. You wanna get me out there in the ocean with the water bouncing all around, and I'm inside some small-ass porthole? Aw, hell no! We still having nightmares about that shit from slavery days."

Janeia grinned. He was grossly overreacting. So she decided to play to his ego.

"I wouldn't think you were afraid of anything," she told him.

He said, "Oh, yeah? Well, what are you afraid of?"

"Of losing you," she responded on beat.

Molasses took another look into her eyes. He wanted to create some mental space between them.

He said, "Look, ah, you gon' have to relax on that

voodoo sauce a little bit, all right? I mean, I know you care
about me and all of that, but *damn.*"

He said, "I told you you got strong game already, just
don't overdo it."

"But it's not a game to me. I love you," she confessed.
"And I think about you all the time."

The chick was outright going for it. She was putting her
emotions all on the line for him.

Molasses had to freeze the breeze for a minute. He
looked into her eyes again, with the water of Lake Michigan rolling in even waves behind her.

He responded to her rather harshly.

"Don't bullshit me, girl. You walkin' in dangerous terri-
tory right now."

But Janeia stood her ground. She meant it.

She said, "Do I look like I'm bullshittin' you? You tell
me. Am I lyin' to you? *Am I?*"

She looked all soft in the eyes, as if she could cry at any moment. Her look was so real that Molasses backed down from
his cold stance. He then held her head in the palm of his
hands and read into her honest face. The young chick had
fallen overboard for him. He could clearly see that now. So he
settled on kissing her lips to calm the tension between them.

Janeia slipped her arms around him and held on for dear
life. And after their kiss, Molasses held her there and stared
out at the water, with Janeia burying her pretty head into
his hard chest.

He mumbled, "I got a solo job to do this weekend. I'll
see you again when I get back on Monday."

Janeia spoke into his chest.

"Just come back to me in one piece."

Molasses grinned. He thought to himself for once that
maybe he had found the one, the one woman who would

love him through hell in search of a heaven. And that reality scared him.

Sometimes it's easier to search for treasure than to find
it. Because finding it forces you to make decisions about
what to do with it. And it makes you fear the reality of how
hard it may be to keep it without becoming a slave to it.

You know, it's funny how so many of us women attempt to delude ourselves into believing that we're the only one in a man's life. . . . But I was pretty much sold on that illusion.

On an early morning within the state of Indiana, a white Ford Taurus rental car with Illinois license plates headed south on Interstate 65.

Charlie, young, white, and innocent-looking, was cruising along comfortably while whistling his favorite songs. He had a long drive to Miami, Florida, to carry out their next contract killing. It was his job to make sure that Molasses got the tools and help he needed to close the deal. So Charlie would take the long drives, loaded with the necessities, while Molasses flew into the locations like a legitimate businessman. And it was a real grind on the road for Charlie, but hell, it paid like a motherfucker. That's why he was whistling while he drove.

THAT night, on a hotel balcony in Miami, Molasses put his clutch moves on the sassy young woman he had met in Chicago, the sweet, chocolate brown one who had been taking the heat from her thugged-out boyfriend over a drug deal that had gone wrong.

Her name was Annette. She was twenty-three, and Molasses had flown her into Miami to give her a little get-away. All she had to do was treat him right.

However, the chick appeared hesitant to accept his advances at the moment.

"This is crazy," she commented. "I've never done anything like this before."

She barely knew his ass. But it was too late for that. Molasses had already flown her in for a good time.

He said, "You want me to stop and fly you back home to Chicago?"

His shit was already hard as he held her from behind. He was in need of her wet softness. And what woman would want to fly back home from a top-of-the-line hotel balcony, overlooking the Miami beaches, while a sexy-ass man was making strong moves on her? She'd be a stiff-ass chick to deny the movement. Some chicks out there were. But not this one.

She shook her head and smiled it off.

"No."

"Well, stop complaining and enjoy this vacation," he told her.

She said, "I mean, it's just that . . ."

Molasses spun her around to face him, and shut her mouth with a teasing kiss on her lips. He gave her just enough of his tongue to make her want it before he pulled away.

The chick grinned and relaxed in his arms, beginning to enjoy the moment. Then they squeezed each other, face to face, eye to eye, and both knowing what they wanted.

Molasses asked her, "You ever hold a loaded gun?"

The chick didn't flinch.

"As a matter of fact, I have," she answered him.

"Did you shoot it?"

She shook her head.

"Fortunately, no."

They continued to read each other's eyes, still awaiting the moment of physicalness.

Molasses said, "Well, I'm loaded right now. And you're holding me like you mean it. . . .

"You wanna get shot?" he joked to her with a pause.

She chuckled at it.

"Oh, my God. I've heard everything now."

Molasses remained cool and calm. It was time to go to work on her alluring body.

"But have you *felt* everything?" he asked her. It was a loaded question.

She meditated on it. She tried to figure out its meaning before she ran her mouth off with too fast of an answer.

"No . . . I can't say that I have."

Molasses backed up slowly and extended his right hand to her. Annette took his hand in hers and followed him back into the bedroom, where the king-size bed awaited them.

Molasses led her over to the lamp and clicked off the lights; only the moonlight was left to highlight their deep brown silhouettes in the dark.

"Are you gonna stop me from doing this?" Molasses teased again as he tugged slowly on her clothes.

"No," she answered him again.

She wore a floral-design wrap dress, strictly for the Florida heat. And her curves stretched that motherfucker to capacity, forcing Molasses to damn-near peel it off of her.

Annette laughed as he struggled with it.

"I need to just use a pair of scissors," he joked to her.

Her dress dropped freely to the floor as she joked back to him.

"Or you could use your teeth."

Molasses raised his brow.

"That would have been interesting. But it's too late for that now," he told her.

Annette stood butt-naked in the middle of his hotel suite, with all her curved, brown splendor wide open for him to explore.

She said, "You can still use your teeth in all the right places . . . as long as you don't use them hard enough to leave a mark on me."

Molasses stood tall and looked into her eyes to read if she was serious. And she was.

"Sounds like you like it wild," he commented. Not that he didn't; he was just being observant.

"I'll take it how I can get it," she answered.

Molasses undid his own clothes, a loose, sky blue silk shirt and beige slacks.

Annette reached out and grabbed his shit in both her hands as soon as he freed it from his boxer shorts.

"Damn," he commented. "You're a little eager, ain't you?"

She grinned at his silhouette in the dark.

"What can I say? You got me hot."

Molasses kept his cool with her, even as she massaged his hard cock in her gentle fingers.

He said, "I thought it was just the Miami heat doing that to you."

"Uh-unh," she grunted before she sunk to her knees to taste him.

Molasses was caught off guard by it. He reached out to caress the back of her head and to steady the impact of his pleasure from her lips and tongue.

"Aww, shit, girl," he moaned to her.

The chick had thawed out his ice in two moves. And once she had him all hot and bothered, Molasses pulled her

well-curved ass over to the bed to give her the wood from
behind, where he could admire her curves and give her
what she needed.

Annette squirmed and moaned as she backed that thing
up, making sure Molasses hit all of her right spots. And did
he ever!

He gave her the best rush of an orgasm that she had ever
experienced.

"*Ooohh, yeeaaahh!*" she squealed.

But Molasses said nothing. He concentrated on control-
ling his delivery. He wanted to make the feeling last. He
knew that making it last as long as possible was how you
truly turned a woman out. And turning her out was what he
was after.

WHEN they were finished with their Miami heat, Molasses eyed the clock on the hotel nightstand. The time
read 11:19 PM. He was tired, but he still had a job to do, and
Miami was known as an all-night party town.

He looked over at Annette, who had exhausted her ener-
gies for the night. Molasses had worn her hot ass out with
his urgent humping.

Nevertheless, he asked her, "You feel like checking out
Miami's nightlife?"

She looked at him as if he was joking.

"I don't think I have enough energy left for that."

Molasses nodded but had no choice. He had to leave the
chick in the room then.

He responded real easy.

"Well, you have a good rest!"

He then climbed out of the bed to re-dress.

"Wait a minute. You're just gonna *leave* me here?" she
asked him.

She was shocked by it. That motherfucker had some real nerve to try and leave her in the hotel room by herself while he went out to party.

Molasses said, "That's your decision," and left it at that.

Annette was not willing to be left alone that night. So she climbed her ass on up.

"I'm coming," she huffed.

Molasses grinned and joked, "I thought you did that a few times already."

She caught on to his joke and grinned back to him.

"Smart-ass."

BY midnight, Charlie's white Ford Taurus rental car had finally made it to Miami. He yawned and read his navigation map from his laptop in the passenger seat. He then exited I-95. His destination was Club Arrival, a popular Cuban nightspot.

INSIDE Club Arrival, a swinging hip-hop song pounded through the speakers. Urban American music had apparently infiltrated every culture.

The Latin mark on Molasses's kill list was front and center on the dance floor. He was having himself a great time with a sexy Latin dance partner.

"This club is piping hot!" he launched into the young woman's ear. "Tell your boss I want to buy this place."

He was dressed in an open-collared red floral shirt with dress slacks and blue alligator shoes. She was in a colorful one-piece dress that teased more than a few men. And she danced like the Latin mommas often did, rapidly twisting and shaking, with plenty of sex appeal. She was one of several hot Cuban girls employed by the owner to keep the party lively with provocative dancing.

She shook her head and told him, "He'll never sell it," referring to her boss, the club owner.

The Latin mark began to eye her slippery curves and asked her, "What about you? Are you for sale tonight?"

The Latina responded with attitude.

"Watch yourself. You know the rules in here."

He ignored the shit and pulled her into his solid belly.

"To hell with the rules!" he piped.

She began to break away, but he grabbed her arm.

"Where are you going?"

She yanked her arm away from him.

"Get your hands off of me!"

Two big-bodied bouncers looked over in their direction. The Latin mark let the woman go. And as soon as she was free, she headed straight for the backroom to tell the boss on his ass.

Inside the owner's office at the back of the club, a slim and stately Latin man in his early forties was smoking a Cuban cigar at his desk when the sexy club dancer barged in on him and broke his cool.

"Raoul, that asshole is at it again! Every time he comes here he treats everyone like *shit*!"

Raoul Benitez, the club owner, was real calm about it. He was not going to let her ranting destroy his expensive cigar moment.

"Who are you talking about?" he asked her.

"Miguel. He's out there fucking off again."

The boss nodded to her slowly.

"I'll handle it."

BACK out at the nightclub entrance, Molasses walked through the door with Annette at his side and checked the place out. He wore a dark sports jacket and slacks with a burnt orange cotton shirt. Annette had tossed her curve-hugging floral dress back on.

"Damn! It looks like we picked the right place," Molasses told her. He was impressed. Club Arrival was packed wall to wall and jumping.

Annette frowned off his excitement.

"Yeah, if you like a bunch of Jennifer Lopez music," she commented.

Molasses smiled at the thought.

He said, "She's fine with me. And I *know* she likes it extra *brown* sometimes," he joked.

Annette frowned again before she broke away toward the restroom.

"I have to go pee," she told him.

"Like I need to hear that," he responded as she headed off through the crowd.

Molasses searched through the club solo for his mark.

AT the long bar area, Miguel was bragging to the bartender about his creative management value.

"The songs from all of the talents that I manage are what make this place happen every night. I deserve more respect in this place. I want to be a part owner. You tell Benitez."

He looked gassed up on alcohol already. He was leaning nearly sideways at the bar counter.

Raoul Benitez appeared on cue from behind him. He had his two big-bodied Latin bouncers in tow. And he was still smoking his cigar.

"Tell me what?" he asked, overhearing the tail end of the conversation.

"I want to buy this place," the unruly mark commented.

The boss told him calmly, "How many times do I have to tell you? The club is not for sale."

•••

FROM the center of the dance floor, Molasses finally spotted him. The Latin mark was standing at the bar in a heated
conversation with two bouncers flanking him. Molasses
smiled, expecting to see some action.

He caught Annette on her way back from the restroom
and informed her of the drama.

"Looks like things are about to get wild up in here."

She looked at him in confusion.

"What are you talking about?"

Back over at the bar area, Miguel was getting loud with
the club owner and his goons.

"Are you throwing me out?" he asked them. He leaned as
he stepped away from the bar to face them.

The boss told him civilly, "I didn't want to have to do this,
Miguel, but you have to learn how to treat nice people."

The irritated Latina dancer watched in the background.
Miguel spotted her there and figured she had been the one
to complain about him.

"What, do you want me to apologize to her?" he asked.
He stretched and grabbed his drink from the bar.

Benitez nodded to him calmly, still with his cigar in
hand.

"Yeah, that would be nice," he commented.

"Okay," Miguel agreed. He looked in the dancer's direction and flashed a middle finger with his free hand. "Fuck
you!" He wasn't bowing down to some nightclub dancer.

He then looked back to Benitez to see how he and his
goons would respond to it.

"How about that apology?" he asked the club owner with
a smirk.

BACK out on the dance floor, Molasses grinned as the club's
owner backed away to allow his bouncers to handle things.

The mark immediately backed up and took a boxing stance away from the bar.

The first bouncer threw an overhand right. But even inebriated, Miguel was able to dodge it and land a body blow to the bouncer's ribs. The second bouncer moved in quickly, but not quickly enough. Miguel clocked him as well. Molasses began to wonder if the man's drunken stance had been only an act.

The mark continued to embarrass the two bouncers in the middle of the club. It was basically a free boxing match.

Benitez then called for backup from his armed security.

OUTSIDE in the club parking lot, Charlie pulled up in his white Taurus. He spotted Molasses's blue Ford Explorer rental with Florida plates from the Miami airport. Molasses had called him about it earlier.

Charlie crept out of his vehicle to leave Molasses the black carrying bag that held the silencer gun and the cell phone for the glove compartment. The Explorer's back door was left unlocked for the drop-off.

BACK inside the club, two armed security men rushed toward the bar area. Miguel noticed the escalating ruckus and decided to move before they unloaded him, especially since he had traveled to the club alone that night.

Everyone made room for the unruly man to make his exit from the club. He was ruining their festive evening.

As he passed by, Molasses nodded to him. He was impressed with his boxing skills.

But the mark ignored him and kept walking.

MIGUEL stepped outside of the club and continued to talk shit as he walked away. Benitez and his armed men followed him out, unfazed by his mouth. Molasses walked out with them, followed by Annette.

"Hey, Benitez, I think you could use some real badasses like me to work at your place," Miguel boasted. "Maybe I'll give you the phone numbers to a few of my cousins and homeboys," he joked, referring to the easily disposed of bouncers.

The unarmed bouncers walked outside only to hear him talking more shit about them.

He said, "Your guys are big, but they fight like pussies with g-strings."

Molasses laughed at the joke himself, and he did it loudly enough to be noticed. He wanted to bring some attention to himself. The crowd all stopped and turned to look in his direction.

Miguel looked in his direction and spat, "Hey, mind your fuckin' business, Black. If I owned this club you wouldn't even be allowed in here."

He looked at Molasses's lady and added, "You or your whore."

Annette gave him a livid tongue right back.

"Yeah, well, fuck you, too!" she told him.

Molasses only smiled. Then he began to take off his sports jacket for a rumble.

INSIDE the Ford Taurus, Charlie looked out the window at the commotion at the club's front entrance and couldn't believe his eyes. Molasses was out there at the center of attention. Charlie was pissed!

"What the hell is he doing?" he grumbled to himself.

MOLASSES was in front of the club talking shit himself, just so he could get into a fistfight to test his own boxing skills. He wanted to call Miguel out.

"See that. Now you've called for round number three," he told the Latin mark.

He had seen Miguel take out the two bouncers inside the club, and Molasses realized now that the man was far from drunk. In fact, despite his mouth, Miguel was rather clever. He could see how the man could muscle young performers out of their money and force his will on them. So Molasses figured he would enjoy taking him apart.

"Well, come on with it, nigga. You can get some," the mark told him.

Benitez and his men decided to watch the scene as if they were all at the fights.

Molasses and Miguel squared off in boxing stances in front of the crowd.

Molasses said, "I'll give it to you south-of-the-border brothers, Sammy. Under one hundred and forty pounds, y'all the shit. But once you get above a hundred and fifty . . ." He stopped and shook his head. "That's it, homes. It's 'Niggatime,'" he boasted.

Miguel responded, "Shut your fuckin' big lips and fight. And I'll make them fatter for you."

Molasses moved right in, with superior speed. Miguel threw some good, strong punches—he just couldn't catch up to connect them. Molasses was in and out, left and right, anticipating every move. He even teased his mark about it.

"You too fucking slow, Sammy. What's that, from too many pinto beans and sipping on tequila?"

The mark grew furious.

He shouted, "My name ain't no fuckin' Sammy! And I'm no fuckin' Mexican."

Molasses told him, "It don't matter to me. You wouldn't care if I was Jamaican."

Maybe Miguel thought of himself as a pure Spaniard. But he didn't look it. He had brown, native traits all over him; with small, dark eyes, a long nose, extra-thick hair, and swarthy skin.

And he was still spiteful, too.

"Fuck all of you!" he yelled.

Annette finally added her piece to the drama. She was just tired of hearing the man's disrespectful mouth.

She screamed, "Kick his fuckin' ass, Moe!"

Miguel responded right back to her.

"Fuck you, you black bitch!"

Molasses went to work on him after that, wearing his ass out from all angles, while Benitez and his men looked on and enjoyed it.

IN the background, two Miami police cruisers pulled into the parking lot to check on the commotion.

Charlie watched them carefully while still staring in disbelief from his rental car. He then began to panic.

"Shit! Now what if they try to arrest him for this?" he mumbled to himself.

With no time to waste, Charlie crept out from his rental car to retrieve the gun bag from Molasses's Explorer.

AT the fight scene, the first white officer walked up calmly to stop the bullshit. He responded as if it was no big deal to him.

"Okay, what's your story tonight, Miguel?"

By then, the mark was all bruised up from Molasses's handiwork on his face.

He said, "I don't know this fuckin' spade. He just comes out of no-fuckin'-where to fight me."

Benitez stepped in to comment on behalf of his club.

"That's not true," he said. "He disrespected his lady. Called her a black whore. So he had to protect her honor."

The second white officer walked up shaking his head at the whole fiasco as the crowd continued to look on.

He said, "You know, guys like you should never have any

money, Miguel. Because I'm real tired of having to lock you up every other weekend just to see you walk with penalties and fees. Because they obviously don't teach you anything."

Miguel laughed as they put the handcuffs on him. He was headed on another ride to the clink.

He boasted, "That's the American way, Officers. The rich can buy their freedom back."

The first officer looked back at Molasses.

"All right, move it along. There's no charges on you," he told him.

Molasses said, "Thanks, Officers. You have no idea how good that sounds to a black man in Florida. I haven't heard good things about this place for us."

"Yeah, well, just move along before we change our minds," the second officer responded as he led his usual suspect toward the squad car.

INSIDE Charlie's rental car, he gently closed his door after retrieving the gun bag. He took a few deep breaths and watched the scene defuse. He then drove off real slowly down the road.

MOLASSES made it back to his own rental with Annette and climbed in. Not long after they had hit the road, the cell phone rang from inside the glove compartment.

Molasses stretched past Annette to pull the phone out.

"I could have gotten that for you," she told him.

He ignored her. The cell phone was not for her to get.

"Yeah," he answered. He knew who it was.

Charlie said, "Can I please talk to you? Alone?"

Molasses told him, "I'll call you right back."

He hung up the phone and pulled over inside a gas station. He climbed out of the car planning to call Charlie back with more privacy away from the girl.

He then leaned back into the Explorer.

"Go inside and get yourself something to snack on. I have to make this phone call," he advised his young date.

She said, "Okay," and climbed out to leave him be.

WHILE holding his cell phone in hand and awaiting the call back from Molasses, Charlie pulled into the same gas station and parked away from him.

Molasses made the call anyway.

"What exactly were you doing back there?" Charlie asked him.

Molasses walked right toward Charlie's rental car as he spoke into the cell phone.

"I was keeping up my skills," he answered.

"Well, how about finding another time to do it?" Charlie snapped at him.

Molasses reached his partner's rental car and hung up the phone again. He spoke to Charlie face-to-face and sternly through the driver's-side window. He didn't appreciate the white boy raising his voice to him.

He said, "Look here, Charlie. You work for *me*. I don't work for you. You got that? It's my ninety percent to your ten—unless you want to start killing these motherfuckers your damn self. And if you're thinking about quittin' me, just remember, you owe me one."

Charlie backed down from the argument.

He stated calmly, "I'm just saying, Moe, that was two hundred fifty thousand *dollars* that you just boxed away. We can't get to this guy in *jail*."

Molasses responded calmly back to him.

"He'll be out soon." Then he smiled. "That's the American way, the rich can buy their freedom," he mocked their mark. "And we'll just get him at his house."

•••

AT the gas station's store entrance, Annette walked out with a bag full of goodies, like a damn kid with an allowance that she couldn't wait to spend.

She then looked around in search of Molasses as if she was lost.

Charlie spotted her from his front window. He then asked his womanizing partner, "What about the girl?"

Molasses looked back to her himself.

"She'll be flying back to Chicago the first thing tomorrow morning," he decided.

Charlie nodded to him.

He said, "All right. Let's wait for our man to get out, and I'll knock out his security system."

CHARLIE started his ignition and drove off. Molasses walked back to his rental.

Inside the Explorer his little lady just smiled at him.

"You remind me of like, a classic tough guy. You just ride into places and beat people down," she told him.

Molasses smiled back to her.

He said, "Yeah . . . and I get the girl, too."

THAT morning, while outside of a plush mansion in the Miami suburbs, Charlie worked diligently to break the security codes with his sophisticated laptop computer.

The place was heavenly. It was all earth tones, with tan walls, white columns, marble, fourteen-foot ceilings, rooms to spare, an interior balcony, and plenty of elegance and style.

A WHILE later, Miguel headed inside the tall black gates behind the wheel of a white Mercedes coupe, wearing the same clothes from the night before.

After parking his Mercedes inside his six-car garage, filled with his other toys—a red Lamborghini, a yellow Hummer, a black Porsche, a white Ferrari Modena, and a classic blue Ford Mustang—Miguel walked into his elaborate home and spotted the black man who had whipped his ass the night before. He was sitting patiently at the bottom of the staircase. He wore a pair of black leather gloves with a silencer gun in hand.

Miguel stopped and stared with wide eyes.

Molasses shook his head and smiled. He said, "This is a bangin'-ass pad, Sammy. It makes my place look like shit. Can I rent a room here?"

Miguel was surprised as hell, but was still filled with enough anger to curse him.

"Fuck you want from me?" he asked him. "You came here to rob me? Why don't you earn your living like I did?"

"Oh, I am earning it, Sammy. I'm being paid real well for this," Molasses told him. "And I hear that you've been taking advantage of your talent. People who can't fight back."

Miguel looked at the silencer gun in his hand. Then he looked up on the walls for his security cameras.

"Oh, don't worry about them cameras. They're not recording anything. That was the second thing that we fucked up. Right after we jammed up your alarm system."

Miguel finally began to panic. He looked around as if he was expecting someone to come and save him.

"What are you looking for now, your guards? Your peoples?" Molasses asked him. He was having his usual good time with the killing.

He began to smile with shiny white teeth, projecting pure confidence.

He said, "I don't think your guys knew you were getting out so soon, man. When I walked up in here, they were all

having a good time out at your pool. So I said, 'Fuck it' and
gave them an extended swim.

"You don't mind, do you, Sammy?"

Miguel had had enough! If he was going to meet his
maker, then he was going to do so like a man!

"Fuck you and your black whore mother!" he spat, just to
get a last rise out of his black tormentor.

Molasses nodded to him calmly.

"Those'll be your last words," he told him.

He then filled his mark's body with bullet holes from the
silencer gun.

Theessrrpp!
Theessrrpp!
Theessrrpp!
Theessrrpp!
Theessrrpp!
Theessrrpp!
Theessrrpp!

The Latino went down still holding on to his bravado.
He took each shot with his fists balled up and with no
screams or begging.

MOLASSES stood over yet another dead body.

He shook his head and looked around the fabulous
Florida mansion in wonder.

"Damn," he commented. "I wonder who inherits this
big-ass crib now."

BACK out at the pool area, three dead Latino guards floated
in bloodied water.

And eventually, we come face-to-face with the truth.

Back on the Chicago streets near midtown, Molasses's brown Bentley was parked at the curb. Inside the car with him was Annette, who had awaited his return from Miami. She wasn't too pleased with him that night either.

"I don't like how you just sent me back home by myself like that," she snapped at him.

Molasses was thoughtful.

He said, "You want to sit here and bitch? I told you I had some extra business to take care of. Now I thought you understood that."

He had no patience for dramatic shit from his women. So he was putting this new broad on notice quick.

She said, "I *do* understand, but that don't mean I have to *like* it."

Down the street from where Molasses was parked, a Chicago police cruiser eased around the corner. At the wheel was Officer Barrett again. What a coincidence?

He drove by and eyed Molasses just to let him know that he was watching him. He figured there must have been some reason why he kept spotting him around the big windy.

•••

MOLASSES caught the officer's meddling stare but
ignored it. He went right back to reprimanding his sassy
young lady.

"Look, if you're gonna be involved with me, then you
have to be mature about certain things. Because I can't have
no damn kids on my hands—"

"I'm not a damn kid," she cut him off and told him.

"Well, stop acting like one then. And watch your damn
tongue while you're at it. That's what gets you into trouble."

Annette sat silently. But Molasses wasn't finished with
her yet.

"I told you before you called me. When you ready for a
real man, *then* call. If you can't handle shit like a real *woman*,
then you shouldn't have called me," he told her.

There was only silence from her.

Molasses followed up and said, "Am I talking to myself in
here, or do you understand me?"

Annette nodded to him obediently.

"I understand you."

"Good."

THAT same night on a public bus, Janeia and her girl Brenda
rode home from the movies. Janeia was still munching a box
of movie popcorn.

Brenda said, "Girl, we need to do this more often. Just
hang out however we have to and spend quality girl time
together. Especially since I don't have no man right now,"
she joked.

Janeia laughed and looked out the window. And lo and
behold, she spotted Molasses sitting with some new chick in
his Bentley. Brenda, however, had her back turned and
missed it.

Janeia stared into the car as Molasses pushed the sharp-
ened nail into the ugly coffin by kissing the woman's lips
before she climbed out of his car. She then walked toward a
black Acura parked in front of the Bentley.

Janeia watched the whole scene with not a word to
Brenda. She didn't even blink. But emotionally, she was
ripped the hell up.

Just when she thought the shock was over, Brenda caught
a glimpse of the final scene herself.

"Oh, shit. Ain't that . . ."

She didn't bother to finish her sentence. They both realized what was going on. The motherfucker had been caught
red-handed out on the prowl.

Janeia took a deep breath and looked away.

WHEN they reached Brenda's apartment, Janeia was still
silent. She prepared herself for a sleepover on a futon bed
inside Brenda's second bedroom.

Brenda stood at the doorway, locked in her thoughts.
What could she say about what they had witnessed to make
it right?

"So what are you gonna do, Janeia? Another one bites
the dust, or what?" she asked.

Janeia stared blankly at the plain white wall in front of
her.

"I don't want to talk about it," she mumbled. And she
meant it. She had some thoughts on her mind that she
needed to negotiate alone.

Brenda understood her friend's dilemma. How could she
not? Janeia had been through the same shit countless times
before. So she gave her girl the needed space to think
things through, and walked out of the room.

As soon as Brenda left her alone, Janeia called Molasses

on his car phone. And instead of fighting fire with fire she decided to go the other route. She would spray water on the issue and give Molasses another shower of love. What sane man could turn down that much love. Even after she had caught him out there with another bitch.

INSIDE the Bentley, Molasses was busy with Charlie going over new contract options. They were looking at more photos and background information printouts.

Charlie told him, "These are all under a hundred thousand." Then he smiled. "No rich people want anyone killed this week."

Molasses said, "Yeah, well, maybe I need to take off for a while anyway."

Charlie nodded in agreement with the idea.

"That's fine with me."

Molasses became concerned with that answer. It came a little too quickly for him.

He said, "You're not getting cold feet on me, are you, Charlie? I'm still one of the baddest hit men you gon' find out here, man. And if you stay good to me, I'll stay good to you."

He said, "I know how good you are at your shit, and you know how good I am at mine."

Charlie was hesitant to speak his mind.

He said, "Yeah, I know, but it's . . . it's just a few things that—"

Molasses's car phone rang and interrupted his partner's stammering comments. Molasses answered it.

"Hey, baby. I miss you. Can't wait to see you. Are you missing me?"

It was Janeia. He hadn't completely forgotten about her, he just had some new meals on the stove. And whenever he had a new chick in his life, Molasses tended to sidestep the old ones. Janeia Goode was an old chick now. Nevertheless, she sounded so loyal.

Molasses smiled and put her on the stereo system where Charlie could hear her. He told Charlie to keep quiet with a finger to his lips.

"Yeah, I'm just gettin' back in town," Molasses spoke into his car phone system. "I got some loose ends to tie up, and I'll make sure to see you right after that."

"How many loose ends?" Janeia asked him.

Molasses decided to charm her.

"Now what did I tell you about all of them questions?" he responded lightly.

She said, "I'm sorry. But I just need you to answer one of them for me before I can go to bed tonight."

Molasses paused and looked over at Charlie.

"What's that?" he quizzed her.

Janeia said, "Well, you already know how much I love you and, you know . . . I just want to know if you love me?"

He decided to be very careful with his words.

"Yeah, I've been thinking about that myself," he told her. "But we gon' have to have that conversation face-to-face. That's not the kind of thing we can discuss over the phone."

She said, "I'm not pressuring you, am I? I don't mean to. I mean, it's just that—"

Molasses cut her off and said, "Nah, you don't have to explain. Like you said, you love me. But I think I need a little more time. Loyalty is not something we can judge overnight," he told her. "Some people run hot and cold. I don't need that shit. I need all warm water. You feel me on that?"

She said, "I feel you on everything. I told you that already. Just make sure you find some time for me. That's all I'm asking."

Charlie gave his partner a look of concern and shook his head. He had heard enough.

Molasses said, "I can do that. But right now I gotta go."

"Okay. Bye, baby," Janeia hummed to him.

"Yeah, I'll see you around," he responded to her with little conviction.

As soon as they hung up, Charlie had some choice words of wisdom for his partner.

He said, "Moe, that right there needs to stop."

Molasses only laughed at him.

"Yeah, she got it bad for me, don't she?"

"If you ask me, I would say that that was a little unstable," Charlie answered.

Molasses raised his brow.

"What do you mean by that?"

Janeia seemed perfectly stable to him. She was a little pressed, but plenty of his women had been that way. And he had been able to work his game with each and every one of them.

But Charlie continued with his concerns. He had some thoughts on his mind about the girl.

"She sounds *too* calm about it," he assessed. "Most women lose their marbles if they even *think* a man is screwing them. Or maybe that's just been from my experiences," he confessed with a grin.

"That's because you don't have no fuckin' *game*, Charlie," Molasses told him. He grinned and said, "Every woman is different. When you get around enough of them, you'll find that out."

Charlie said, "Yeah, well, I'll tell you again, you need to stop mixing them with our business."

Molasses paused.

"Look, Charlie," he said, "let me explain something to you. Women are my thing. I understand them. Okay? And for a lot of women, they've been told since birth not to fuck with the cookie jar. And what I mean by the cookie jar, is bad motherfuckers like me."

He said, "Now everybody tells them, 'Don't mess with that guy.' But that's like pouring kerosene on the fire for a lot of women. Especially the *fine* ones. Because they want what they want. *Always.*"

Charlie nodded, agreeing with him.

"Obviously," he said.

Molasses continued:

"So all of these women that I deal with, Charlie, they know exactly what they're gettin' into. And if they don't, I explain it to them. They all know my rules. So don't cry no tears for 'em, Charlie, because they don't deserve none.

"They're all big girls now," he told him. "And they choose who they wanna choose."

Then he smiled at his partner.

"And when I get 'em, Charlie . . . I get 'em *good.*"

Charlie sat back in the plush leather seat and grinned, while Molasses gloated on his skills with women. And like he said, he was good at that shit; as good as he was at killing.

BACK at Brenda's apartment, Janeia stretched out on a futon and continued to stare into empty space. She wondered what her next move would be if Molasses was indeed playing her for a fool. She had been strung out over bad boy players too often, and she was running out of patience for it. So she figured that maybe she'd try more drastic measures this time to solve her man problems. For instance, what would Molasses do if it was him, if he was the woman?

Brenda snuck a peek in the room at her girl, and Janeia failed to even notice it. She was much too deep into her thoughts. So Brenda shook her head and continued on her way to the kitchen for a late-night snack. She had heard a whisper or so of Janeia's phone conversation with her cheating-ass man, but she dared not comment on it. Her girl would just have to work out her love demons on her own. She never listened much to logical advice anyway. Janeia made all of her own decisions, good or bad. But lately they were mostly bad.

I wouldn't wish anything bad on him. I love him. I really do. But like they say, "What goes around, comes around."

On another night on Chicago's South Side, Molasses cruised the streets in his Bentley. He was really feeling the car and his life. And who wouldn't? The man was on top of things.

He talked into his car phone, connected through the stereo system, with another one of his women. He had taken time off from killing men to spend more time as a lady-killer in the bedroom.

"I gotta check my schedule to see when I can see you again," he told his lady. "You know, I'm not just sitting on my hands around here."

The woman responded to him in the sweetest voice, "Well, just let me know."

"Oh, no problem," he assured her.

He hung up the phone and turned his CD player back on. A swinging, big bass R&B song filled the car through the top-of-the-line speakers.

Molasses was enjoying his late-night cruise and music so much that he failed to notice the burgundy GMC sedan that was speeding toward him from his left. With full intention, the burgundy sedan crossed the yellow traffic median and smashed into the driver's side of Molasses's Bentley.

Bllooomm!

The Bentley absorbed most of the impact, but it was pushed into the cars that were parked on the right.

Crraaasshh!

Two brown gunmen dressed in black jumped out of the sedan and began to riddle Molasses's treasured ride with bullets from assault weapons.

Tat-tat-tat-tat-tat-tat-tat-tat . . .

It was a reckless scene. They didn't even care about witnesses.

A third gunman watched from the backseat of the sedan, and shook his head at his amateurish partners. He then stepped out of the car with a black nine-millimeter pistol in hand. He boldly walked up to the Bentley to finish off the job the right way, at close range. You don't just shoot up a motherfucker's car and expect him to die. You put a bullet in his ass up close, like Molasses would do if *he* was on the job.

But as soon as the lead gunman reached the driver's-side window of the wrecked Bentley, Molasses popped him four times with his own gun.

Pop! Pop! Pop! Pop!

Molasses had taken the initial impact of the crash, and then managed to slither into the backseat to cover his position. And it worked. The front seat had been ripped to shreds, but the back was barely touched. And the Bentley was so loaded with expensive equipment that it absorbed the majority of the bullets.

After watching their leader hit the ground with four bullets in his ass from the direction of the wrecked car, the first two gunmen opened fire and riddled the Bentley a second time.

Tat-tat-tat-tat-tat-tat-tat-tat . . .

Neither of them were sure of their technique, so they

planned to *make sure* before their mark fired on either of them.

"I'll take the left side; you take the right," the first gunman told the second.

The second gunman shook his head, unwilling to play the fool.

"Naw, you take the right."

Their right side of the car was the driver's side.

The first gunman got bold about it.

"Fuck it, I ain't scared."

The scattering of witnesses continued to look on from safe distances. But no police cars were yet in sight. So the two gunmen walked up on opposites sides of the Bentley to finish the job.

Molasses anticipated their attack and kicked the driver's-side door open to take out the bolder gunman, who had approached the right side.

He popped him four times like the first.

Pop! Pop! Pop! Pop!

The gunman fell dead in the street not far from his leader.

The last gunman reacted by taking cover and firing his gun at whatever moved near the car.

Tat-tat-tat-tat-tat-tat-tat-tat-tat . . .

Molasses rolled out of the car to safety, and the barrage of aimless bullets all missed him.

The surviving gunman finally retreated, firing continuously in Molasses's direction as he backed off.

Tat-tat-tat-tat-tat-tat-tat . . .

The man ran away with his assault weapon still in hand.

Molasses painfully climbed to his feet. Countless nicks and bruises covered his face and body. He stood crookedly in the street and eyed his totaled Bentley. He was injured and bloodied from the car wreck, but was miraculously untouched by any of the bullets that had been fired at him. He held his nickel-plated pistol dangerously at his side.

"Shit!" he cursed, still eyeing the car wreck. "Somebody gon' pay for this," he promised in a mumble.

BY the time police sirens approached the scene, Molasses was leaning up against his car waiting. He had responded in self-defense, with a licensed gun. And he was in no condition to run and dodge anyone. Besides, he still found it hard to believe that his precious ride had been totaled.

"Shit!" he repeated to himself, still staring at the car.

An older black man walked out from inside of a storefront doorway and shook his head in disgust. It was an ugly wreck of a beautiful ride.

He said, "Damn. You should have been driving a Hyundai, brother."

Molasses looked and forced out a grin to the old man, even though it hurt his face to smile.

Three police cruisers showed up at the scene with several officers hopping out of their squad cars with their guns drawn.

They found Molasses limping around with a battered body, a gun in hand, two stiffs near his feet, several wrecked cars, and a three-hundred-thousand-dollar Bentley that had been riddled by at least thirty bullets.

The police officers surveyed the scene and were not planning on taking any chances with him.

"Drop your weapon and raise your hands!" they shouted immediately.

Molasses did what he was told. The officers moved in to secure his gun from the ground, and made him assume the position of arrest until they could find out what had happened out there.

"Watch my ribs," Molasses told them.

Three officers, two white and one black, all ignored him and waited for more backup. It was a real mess out there, and too many people were beginning to gather.

"Move back," they told the onlookers.

When the back-up squad cars appeared, Officer Barrett was among them, along with four other cars and six other officers.

"It was self-defense," Molasses explained to the arresting officers. "They rammed my car head-on and tried to kill me. I mean, just look at my car," he told them.

"They tried to kill him, all right. I saw everything," the old man informed the officers.

Other witnesses stepped forward and agreed with Molasses's story. It was a cut-and-dry case. The man had defended himself from a very obvious gang of killers.

"Yeah, they were definitely trying to kill him," a young black woman added.

The officers continued with their job without much concern for the witnesses.

"All the information here will be gathered in time. But we're just doing our jobs right now," one of the white officers stated.

Officer Barrett didn't say a word. He inspected the wreckage of Molasses's prized Bentley, and smiled.

Molasses caught the man's familiar face and his open smile and ignored him. The jealous cop was only mad that he could never afford a Bentley. Now he had a chance to laugh about it. Misery loves company.

"Do you have a permit to carry this firearm?" one of the arresting officers asked him. The nickel-plated nine was admired.

Molasses answered, "Yes, I do. It's in my glove compartment."

They inspected the damaged glove compartment inside

the Bentley and pulled out a legitimate firearms permit.

Officer Barrett walked up closer and finally decided to speak. He was still grinning.

"I guess you need some security yourself, Moe-lasses," he teased him. Since their last encounter, Officer Barrett had asked enough questions around the city to find out Warren's street name.

Molasses took note of it and continued to ignore him. Too much of a response either way would have been suspect. The black cop, however, was really beginning to show his ass.

An ambulance showed up at the site next. The officers then escorted Molasses to the ambulance to see about his wounds. They had also reported the two dead bodies.

"You get these wounds checked out, and we'll need to ask you a few more questions later," the officers told him. In the meantime, they held on to his gun for evidence.

"No problem," Molasses assured them. He was then helped into the back of the ambulance.

As the officers continued to inspect the crime scene, two plainclothes detectives showed up.

Officer Barrett took notice of the two white detectives and decided to do some snooping of his own. He approached the older black man who had witnessed every-thing. The old guy was still hanging around the crime scene. He lived there.

"You seen this guy Molasses around before?" Officer Barrett asked him. He spoke Warren Hamilton's street name as if it was common knowledge.

The older man nodded to him.

"Yeah, sure. I've seen 'im."

"Can you tell me what you know about him?"

Officer Barrett spoke to the older black man in the respectable tone of a nephew. He would be honored to receive the information.

The older black man answered, "He got a lot of money." Then he paused. "But I never seen him hustling no drugs or nothing, if that's what you mean. He don't hustle no drugs."

The black cop smiled and nodded back to him.

"So, he has clean money?" he asked.

The older man nodded again.

"Yeah, you can say that. Clean money."

"Okay, what else do you know about him?" the black cop continued. He was on a roll.

The old man cracked a gap-toothed smile.

"He got a lot of women. *Fine* women."

One of the white detectives overheard the tail end of the conversation and butted in to gather information for himself. Questioning witnesses was what he and his partner were there to do.

"What do you think you're doing?" he asked the lower-ranking officer. The other detective was already questioning Molasses at the ambulance.

"Practicing," Officer Barrett answered honestly. He figured he would be moving on to a new position soon, even if it was outside of the police force. He had some ideas he wanted to pursue in his life, and he definitely wanted to make more money.

"Practicing what?" the detective asked him. The man needed to remember what his job description was, to arrest the criminals and serve and protect the citizens, not to collect information toward solving cases. That was a detective's job.

But the black cop answered boldly, "Detective work."

The detective studied the officer's defiant posture before he spoke on it.

"Well, do me a favor, and practice detective work *after* you've become a detective, *Officer.*"

Officer Barrett nodded and backed away. He had already

gathered enough information on Molasses to serve his own purposes.

The detective then approached the same older black man with his own line of questions.

"What can you tell me about this guy, uh," he looked down at his notes and said, "Molasses?"

The detective had done some fast work of his own.

The black man looked at the white detective in utter confusion.

He answered, "Who? Molasses? Somebody named their boy Molasses? I never even heard of him."

Of course, the detective didn't believe the man. He had just overheard him spilling his guts to the black officer. But what else could the detective do? The black man was already walking away to mind his own business. He figured he had said enough already.

By that time, several tow trucks were pulling up to haul away the smashed vehicles, with a second ambulance arriving for the dead bodies. The first ambulance left to take Molasses to the hospital's emergency room for further evaluation of his injuries. They were escorted there by two police cruisers, one in the front and one behind.

Whurrp! Whurrp! Whurrp! Whurrp!

AT the emergency room of Chicago Central Hospital, Ms. Hamilton showed up and made her way through the crowd to find her boy. She looked fabulous as usual. Like her son, Mom had it going on.

Molasses had been allowed to call her regarding his accident and the needed hospital stay. And they were holding him in a small, private room where the two detectives continued to question him.

When his mother had reached them, she found her only

child sitting on a hospital bed with his shirt off, an IV in his arm, bandages wrapped around his ribs and head, and an ice pack applied to his swollen face.

The first detective asked him, "So, you have no idea why anyone would want to kill you?"

Molasses shook his head in obvious pain, right before he spotted his mother.

She barged right through the investigating detectives.

"Oh, my God! What happened, baby? Who did this to you?"

Molasses only stared at her. He knew, before he even called her, how his mother would react to it all. He figured he could use her ranting to his advantage. Nevertheless, her tone did nothing to soothe his throbbing headache.

The second detective took in the mother's expensive dress. She had high-priced clothes, shoes, rings, bracelets, and an impeccable hairdo. She noticed the man staring, and decided to press them about the questions they were asking her son.

"What do you two wanna know? I'll tell you what you *need* to know," she told them. "Ever since Warren was a little boy, growing up on the West Side of Chicago, kids were always picking on him, just because he was black and beautiful. I mean, look at him.

"Just look at him," she told them.

They all looked at Molasses's handsome, dark features and how they had been injured in the attack. Molasses looked straight ahead and grimaced. He was using his mother's show to his advantage, but that didn't mean he had to like the shit.

The detectives looked at each other and were speechless. Ms. Hamilton had managed to back them on their heels. The power of motherhood held them in check. They knew the routine. They had mothers, too. And mothers didn't want to hear about police work.

She said, "And now all of these guys out there are jealous *niggas*, just because he has something. Ain't nothin' but *crabs* in a *barrel*. As soon as my boy works hard and makes something of himself, they only want to bring him back down and hurt him."

The detectives looked at each other a second time before they raised their brows and decided to move on. It became obvious that they wouldn't get much of their work done with the man's obnoxious mother around.

"We'll be back to see you later. All right?" they promised Molasses before they walked out. They left him alone in the room with his mother.

She continued to stare at his injuries.

"Did you get robbed or something?" she asked him.

Molasses shook his head real gently because of the pain.

"Nah, they didn't want to rob me. They wanted to kill me," he told her.

She nodded her head. Then she asked him, "Did you have any money on you?"

Molasses frowned. Didn't he just tell his mother that some folks tried to kill his ass? What did money have to do with anything?

"It wasn't about no money," he told her.

She took in his words and paused.

"Well, how much you got on you, then?"

Molasses couldn't believe his fucking ears! His mother was still sweating money even while he was in the hospital with bruises and bandages from an attempt on his life.

He finally snapped at her and said, "I'm glad you still got your priorities in order."

She ignored him and finally commented on his injuries.

"Well, damn, they messed you up pretty bad, baby. It looks like it's gonna cost a lot to fix you up. You think you'll need plastic surgery? I hear that's expensive," she told him.

"I'm sure glad I got some good black genes," she commented of herself, grinning.

Molasses just stared at her. The woman was impossible. If she wasn't his mother, he wouldn't have the time of day for her. But she *was* his mother. So he had to deal with all of her hypocrisies. And she had to deal with his.

She caught her son's glare and asked him, "What?" as if she had said nothing wrong.

Molasses took a deep breath and dropped his eyes away from her and to the shiny black floor. He had some healing and thinking to do.

A FEW mornings after the attempt on his life, Molasses continued to hobble in pain at his condo on Lakeshore Drive. He made it to his black leather La-Z-Boy chair in the living room and took a seat to enjoy a glass of orange juice. He had been thinking things over for a few days now. His returned pistol from the Chicago police sat out on the coffee table in front of him.

He took a sip of his orange juice and nodded to himself. He needed to call Charlie. He had some plotting to do, and he was now used to Charlie's help.

When his partner in crime answered his phone, Molasses said, "Hey, Charlie, some crazy shit went down a few nights ago."

"Yeah, I heard," Charlie told him. He said, "I figured you'd call me when you were ready. I didn't think you'd take a couple of days to do it, though," he commented. He figured Molasses would have jumped on the horn immediately to fly into counterattack mode.

"Yeah, well, my goddamn head and body was killing me. So I had to chill for a while. They wrecked my ride, too, Charlie," he added.

"Yeah," Charlie responded to him. He realized how attached Molasses had become to the Bentley. It wasn't as if he could jump up and buy a new one like an overpaid athlete or rapper. Molasses had to earn another high-priced ride through blood. Literally.

He said, "I just needed to lay low and relax. But I need your help now. So meet me at our spot by lunchtime," he told his partner.

"All right," Charlie responded.

Molasses hung up the phone and continued to think to himself.

He held his glass of orange juice to his lips and mumbled, "Who could it be? Could it be you, Charlie? . . ."

He shook his head at the thought of it.

"Nah, not Charlie. But just in case." He picked up his nickel-plated nine-millimeter from the coffee table, suspecting anyone.

A WANDERING mind will make an unfocused man or woman try just about anything. And all that Janeia Goode had been able to do since spotting Molasses out on the prowl with another woman was think about tracking him down. He no longer answered her phone calls or returned her messages, and she had no idea where he lived. So if she was desperate to see him and to get to the bottom of things, what choice did she have other than to retrace his steps with the hope of bumping into him somewhere?

The last time she spotted Molasses, more than a week ago, was near midtown, when she and Brenda were returning from the movies. So Janeia rode the same bus obses-

sively, ignoring most of her classes at Chicago State. Until
finally, there he was, cruising past the bus in his black Navigator in the opposite direction.

Janeia noticed him and jumped up out of her seat to
address the bus driver.

"Oh, I just missed my stop. I need to get off. I don't
know what I was thinking."

It was no big deal to the bus driver. They had not started
moving toward the next stop yet. So he reopened the front
doors and let her ass out.

Janeia hit the sidewalk with her school things and began
to sprint down the street as if she would run Molasses down
in his Navigator.

Luckily, a red light stopped him at the next street corner.

Janeia seized the opportunity and dashed out into the
middle of the street to try and get his attention in his
rearview mirror. She waved her hands furiously as she ran,
as if she was a hitchhiker, running for her life from a killer
in the woods. And she succeeded at getting his attention,
but only because Molasses was extra alert now in traffic.

He spotted her in his side-view mirror and began to
frown.

"The fuck is she doin'?" he asked himself. He had no
time for the girl. And since she had no way of knowing
whether he spotted her or not, he waited for the green light
and drove forward as if he hadn't seen her.

"Crazy-ass girl," he told himself as he drove toward his
destination.

Janeia watched his Navigator speed ahead into traffic
and gave up on her chase. Her entire body showed the de-
feat. She dropped her hands to her sides and took a deep
breath. Then she waited for the traffic to stop again so she
could make her way back out of the street from the yellow
median where she stood.

•••

CHARLIE had witnessed the whole scene from his black Volkswagen Bug. He had turned the corner a block behind Molasses's Navigator and less than twenty yards behind Janeia. He had no proof that the young woman was attempting to wave down his womanizing partner with the host of other cars that were on the road. But he did have a strong hunch about it. Molasses had that type of an effect on women. So Charlie took a good look at Janeia for his own mental record as he drove by her.

"Shit!" he told himself as he passed her. "She's a fox."

Then he remembered her.

"Wait a minute. That's the girl Moe took to St. Louis with him."

He nodded to himself, convinced of his own wisdom.

"Moe's gonna get himself in deep trouble sooner or later with these girls. But he just won't listen to me."

MOLASSES waited inside his black Navigator for Charlie to arrive at their meeting place near midtown. It was the same empty block where he had met the new girl, Annette, and had smacked up her punk boyfriend.

Charlie pulled up behind him in his Volkswagen.

Molasses swung open his passenger-side door for Charlie to climb in. Charlie climbed in and immediately checked out Molasses's injuries. It wasn't as if he would heal overnight. He was no superhero after all.

Molasses had his gun on his lap in plain view. He also wore a shoulder-strap holster. He was ready for war.

Charlie nodded to him.

"They got ya pretty bad, huh?"

Molasses nodded back to him, real easy.

"Yeah."

"They towed the Bentley?" Charlie asked him.

"Of course they did," he said. "I couldn't drive the shit."
Then he looked his partner in the eyes for his key question.

"You wouldn't happen to know anything about this hit,
would you, Charlie?"

Charlie was unassuming. He nodded pensively.

He answered, "I'll find out."

Molasses read his calm tone and understood that Charlie
was still his partner. His setup and information man
remained all business.

Molasses nodded back to him and revealed his plan.

"In the meantime," he said, "I got an old friend I need
for us to visit on the West Side."

Charlie looked at him for clarity.

"You mean you need me to do surveillance?"

Molasses answered, "Nah, not this time." He paused and
said, "I need you to carry a gun."

Charlie chuckled nervously.

"But then you would blow my cover," he responded. He
was right.

Molasses told him, "Trust me, Charlie, where we're
going tonight, you can't get much more underground. Your
cover will be just fine."

Charlie was still hesitant.

He said, "I don't know if I like this."

Molasses addressed him sternly.

"You don't have to like it. You just *do* it."

Charlie read the determination on his partner's injured
face and realized that he had no choice. It was time to go
into action.

He took a breath and agreed to it. Then he smiled.

"What's so damn funny?" Molasses asked him.

Charlie declined to let him in on the joke. He was thinking about the girl in the street who was trying to run his
partner down. But he didn't want to bring it up in case

Molasses asked why he was following him. Charlie understood his place. He had as much trust as one could expect
from a hit man. He wanted nothing to cloud their relationship, especially after an attempted hit on Molasses's life. So
he kept quiet about the girl.

He responded, "Nothing," instead. "I'm just thinking
about me holding a gun."

Molasses was thinking about that himself. Charlie was no
killer. He was an underworld deal maker.

Molasses said, "Don't worry about it. I'll do all the
shooting. You just pose with the gun."

Charlie looked at him and chuckled. What else could he
do? Molasses was a real nutcase. And he was already
involved with him.

I imagined that Molasses must have had a painful childhood. And now that he was grown, he was taking his pain out on everyone else.

That night, after his meeting with Charlie, Molasses prepared himself for war.

At his condo, he opened a hidden storage panel in his kitchen ceiling and pulled down assault weapons, shotguns, automatic pistols, leather gloves, bulletproof vests—the *works*—and began preparing for some serious shit.

He selected a couple of assault weapons, and three pistols—one large, two small—and packed them, along with plenty of bullets, into a large black bag. He then put on dark clothes, his bulletproof vest, and a black knit hat before heading for the door.

Molasses drove through the bleak areas of Chicago in a dark sedan, acquired specifically for the night's mission. Who was going to stop the coldhearted vengeance of a man who killed for a living? Somebody was going to die that night. There was no doubt about it.

Molasses made it to the meeting place and waited patiently for Charlie. He even wondered for a second whether the white boy would show. It was a different ball game for Charlie to have to carry a loaded gun. His computer skills couldn't help him with that.

However, Charlie did show, wearing dark clothes and driving a dark sedan himself. He climbed out of the sedan and into his partner's car.

Molasses immediately pointed Charlie in the direction of a second bulletproof vest on the floor.

"Put that on," he told him. "And you carry that."

Charlie looked to the floor and spotted a black bulletproof vest and an assault weapon. He then panicked.

"I don't even know how to use that thing," he bitched. He figured that he would carry a simple pistol. He was already hesitant about Molasses's plans, but it was too damn late to back out.

Molasses responded calmly, "Look, Charlie, I got some loose ends I need to tie up. Just follow my lead."

He wasn't trying to hear shit else. Charlie was in on the deal and that was that.

Molasses smiled and said, "Besides, if we're lucky, you won't even have to use that thing."

"And if we're *not* lucky?" Charlie questioned.

Molasses eyed him seriously.

"Then brace yourself when you fire. That motherfucker's got a hell of a kick to it."

Charlie sat with wide eyes and was nervous as hell.

INSIDE a garage on Chicago's West Side, Kirk Stringer, a slick, streetwise black man in his early forties, joked with three of his younger henchmen. They all watched a taped boxing match of Mike Tyson against Lennox Lewis on a giant TV screen with surround sound.

You could park at least eight cars in the space of their garage. But there were only three cars at the moment: an

old cranberry Cadillac with whitewall tires, a basic Ford
Explorer, and a black-on-black Maxima.

Kirk's first henchman was a fat man in his early thirties
holding a gyro sandwich. The second was a tall, thin dude
in his late twenties, who would have looked at home on a
basketball court. And the third was the wannabe thug
Molasses had smacked up and taken Annette from. He was
still in his early twenties.

"Mike don't even look like himself in this fight, man,"
the tall, thin cat said as he watched.

Kirk responded, "Yeah, 'cause he's getting his ass kicked.
People too used to seeing Mike win."

Kirk then looked over to the fat man, who was busy
munching.

He joked and said, "Hey, Flip, you need to go on a diet
or something, man. Stop eating them damn gyros and
drinking that malt liquor shit."

The tall cat laughed.

"Fuck you laughing at, you long-neck motherfucker?"
the fat man snapped at his slender partner. "Look like a
damn ostrich."

The young thug only smiled and remained silent while
watching the boxing match. After losing his hustle and his
girl over a bum drug transaction, he didn't have much to
talk or joke about.

Kirk said, "Y'all look like the *Fat Albert Show* to me. *Fat
Albert 2000.*"

His men ranged in height, size, and build just like the
popular cartoon characters of the seventies.

The tall, slim one responded, "So, what does that make
you, man?"

Kirk kicked up his feet on his dusty, wooden desk.

Right on cue, he answered, "I'm Bill Cosby, motherfucker. I'm the one who makes the shit happen."

The young thug finally spoke up with something to say. He looked confused.

He asked Kirk specifically, "Bill Cosby had something to do with *Fat Albert*?"

They all stopped and stared at him for a minute. Did that young asshole really ask that question?

Kirk just shook his head.

He said, "You young bloods don't know *shit* out here nowadays. You need a got'damn nigga's history class."

He looked at his other two misfits and added, "The next thing you know, he'll ask me what Jimmie Walker had to do with *Good Times.*"

The older men shared another laugh at the younger man's ignorance.

OUTSIDE of Kirk's garage, Molasses pulled up in the dark sedan with Charlie in the passenger seat. They parked and quietly hopped out of the car.

Molasses told his partner, "Just stay calm, Charlie. Everything's gonna be all right. You hear me?"

Charlie was still shaking in his stance.

"Ah, yeah, sure. Okay," he uttered.

Molasses gave Charlie another look and responded sternly to him.

"At least hold the fucking gun like you *mean it*, Charlie!"

Charlie tightened his grip on the assault weapon. Then they headed toward a side door.

BACK inside Kirk's garage, the men all froze. They watched cautiously as Molasses, with Charlie trailing him, walked right in on their fight party. They all noticed the guns and bulletproof vests and knew this was a serious situation.

Kirk stood slowly from his seat and remained calm. But

his henchmen began to panic, especially the young thug who had previously met up with Molasses.

Molasses immediately took note of him standing there nervously inside the open room. There was nowhere to run or hide.

"Don't I know you from somewhere?" he asked the young thug. Molasses didn't forget many faces. People didn't tend to forget his face, either, nor did they forget his name.

Kirk became protective of his young recruit. The kid had potential; he was just still young and stupid at the moment.

Kirk responded, "Yeah, you know him. You smacked him up and took his lady. So I had to calm him down and let him know who you were."

Kirk smiled to patronize Molasses. He said, "You know, these young bloods today, man, some of 'em don't have respect for their elders."

Molasses nodded to him.

He said, "Yeah, well, three of 'em tried to knock me off a few nights ago. You know anything about that, Kirk?"

It became hard to breathe in there. Kirk noticed Molasses's nicks and scars even through his dark clothes, but he kept his cool about it. There was no sense in kicking a man while he was down. Particularly a vengeful man like Molasses.

He said, "You're not assuming things, are you? And especially not putting *my* name in it."

Molasses said, "You tell me, man. Am I?"

Kirk said, "We go back too long for that shit, Moe. What have we known each other for now, twenty-five, thirty years?"

They had known each other a long time. And at one time Kirk was also *his* elder. But it didn't seem that way once the word on the street got around that Molasses had become a killer for hire. Killers didn't have ages or rank anymore, just prices.

"True," Molasses responded to him. "But then again, the

way I see it, we never really liked each other, we just kept a respectable distance."

Kirk's gun was in the small of his back, and he was thinking about how he could get to it. His young followers thought the same about their guns. Nevertheless, none of them wanted to make any hasty moves.

Molasses continued:

"And you know, I was more of a solo artist. I did my thing on my own," he commented. "But you, you always had collaborators. And if anything went down in Chicago, you knew about it. So I'm here for some answers. 'Cause I know you know something."

Kirk nodded to him carefully.

He said, "That's cool. I can understand that. You're just asking around. But what's with the white boy, man? Why you bring him up in my place? This ain't no multicultural shit in here. No MTV allowed."

Kirk smiled it off, figuring he'd play the humor game to lighten things up. It was at least worth a shot.

By then, Charlie was sweating bullets. He didn't want to hear mention of his presence at all. And it made it worse when Kirk's henchmen began to hold in their laughs toward him. Charlie was beginning to feel slighted.

Molasses responded, "It's a new age now. We all need to diversify. You get more money that way."

Kirk said, "Oh, yeah. Well, more money don't make it good money. And when you diversify, you may make new friends, but sometimes you make new enemies, too."

Kirk took another look at Charlie.

"Maybe your white boy knows something about it," he insinuated. If humor failed to work, he figured he'd play a game of divide and conquer.

Kirk was a crafty old head. You couldn't last in the street game as long as he had without being crafty.

Molasses said, "I asked him already. And he don't know nothing."

Kirk smiled at him.

"Yeah, white boys always claim that shit. They ain't known nothin' for a long-ass time. Lyin' motherfuckers," he spat in Charlie's direction.

Kirk attempted to play up the race card with Molasses. There had been a long history of distrust for white criminals in America. And he felt that Molasses should have known that history. You never side with a white boy over your brothers.

Molasses said, "You wanna ask him yourself?"

Charlie heard that and was in near shock, scared to death. His partner was leaving him out to dry, just to see how he would respond.

Charlie wasn't so sure now if he was the partner or the mark in that room. How much did Molasses really trust him?

Kirk looked at Charlie and launched into a game of old-time street smarts.

He said, "So, it looks like your plan is working, huh, white boy? You get two strong niggas to kill each other over some bullshit and then you pick up the pieces and take it to the bank."

Charlie began to hold in his piss before he wet himself. He then wondered what his own next move would be.

He screamed, "*You're* the fucking liar! I don't even fucking know you!"

He was trying his hardest to sound like a tough guy, but his shaking hands betrayed him.

Molasses looked straight ahead at Kirk and told Charlie, "If he's lying, then you shoot his ass, Charlie. I wouldn't let him lie like that on me."

Kirk didn't like the sound of that. He could tell that the

white boy was scared stiff. Nevertheless, all it took was a squeeze of a gun trigger pointed in the right direction to kill a man. So he changed his approach before the white boy shot him out of pure nervousness. That got'damned Molasses wasn't looking out for his brothers at all. Kirk could clearly see that now.

He said, "What you really come here for, Moe? You know I didn't have shit to do with no hit. That's your kind of business. We all know what you do for a living. And ain't nobody trippin' on you, man. So what's really going on here?"

If all else failed, then the truth will set you free. Or at least Kirk hoped that was the case, because he didn't know a damn thing about Molasses's situation. He had heard about it, but that was it. So he decided to talk pure logic with him.

Molasses eyeballed him with evil intent anyway. He didn't really give a fuck anymore. He knew that Kirk didn't have anything to do with it. He just knew that somebody had to pay, and he never really liked Kirk. So he decided to tell him.

"I just never liked you, Kirk. And I always thought that 'Kirk' was a punk-ass name."

Molasses grinned and joked, "Beam me up, Scotty."

Charlie couldn't help it. He was a big *Star Trek* fan. So he had to hold in his laugh.

Molasses was on a roll in there. And he had everybody scared to move.

He said, "You still think 'Molasses' is a punk-ass name, too. Don't you, Kirk?" he instigated. He wanted to provoke the man into doing something stupid—and fatal.

Kirk finally gave up on it. Molasses was beyond reason. He could read it in his eyes. He was out for blood and there was no stopping him.

Kirk said, "You disappointin' me, man. I always thought you were smarter than that. Out of all the people in the 'hood that we knew, I always thought you was one of the smartest.

"But this right here is a dumb-ass move," Kirk tried to warn him. "This ain't no Clint Eastwood movie, man."

Kirk's henchmen began to ready themselves for a shoot-out. It had become an any-minute deal in there. All they were doing was breathing, sweating, and hoping to make it to another day.

Charlie even secured a better grip on his assault weapon, feeling the tension rising to a peak inside the room.

But Molasses loved it! He thrived under tension. Tension was his element.

He said, "Remember when everybody used to play target practice with their guns, shooting beer cans and wine bottles? I always had the best aim. You remember that, Kirk?"

Kirk listened to him and readied himself to duck.

He said, "Yeah, I remember."

Molasses continued, "Your aim wasn't worth *shit*. You was just a better boxer. Well, I'm a better boxer myself now, Kirk, since y'all in here watching the Mike Tyson fights. But you know what, a lot of people on the streets don't box no more."

Then he paused.

"You get any better at shooting?" he asked his old neighborhood associate.

Kirk forced himself to remain calm.

He said, "I understand that you're a little hot about what went down the other night, man. But don't lose your head. That kind of shit is for youngbloods."

"You mean like him?" Molasses asked of the young thug. He aimed his gun at the boy's chest and fired.

Blauuww!

Kirk and his men found themselves paralyzed as their friend dropped to the floor and struggled to get out his last breath. His chest had been ripped to pieces. They all wanted to move to help him, but that motherfucking Molasses was so crazy with a gun that their bodies betrayed their minds. And the heat in there increased to the boiling point.

Kirk said, "You crazy, man. I'ma pray for you."

But at the moment, he was praying for himself.

The others had had enough of him. They both reached to pull their guns and take cover, but Molasses anticipated their moves and shot them just as Kirk knew he would.

Blop! Blop! Blop! Blop!

Kirk still didn't budge. He knew he was no match for Molasses with a gun. They were practically sitting ducks in there as soon as Moe walked in with his gun drawn. And now Kirk was the last of his men left standing.

Charlie quivered with not one bullet fired from his assault weapon. His finger was frozen on the trigger.

Molasses squared off with Kirk, daring him to try something.

"Let's do it, Kirk. It's me and you now. Let's have a real shoot-off."

Kirk refused, still believing he could talk himself out of the madness somehow.

He said, "I'm not doing it, man. I'm trying to keep my hustle going. I got no beef with you."

"Even after I just popped your whole crew?" Molasses instigated. What kind of underboss would Kirk be if he allowed him to walk into his establishment and kill everyone there and not even *think* about returning the favor one day real soon?

Nevertheless, Kirk shrugged, determined to make it out of there alive.

He explained it logically. "Everybody in the street business gonna die sooner or later. Even *you*, man."

Molasses told him, "Not tonight I'm not."

At least six more of Kirk's henchmen rushed into the

garage right in time to save him. They fired at Molasses and
Charlie, forcing them to take cover.

Pop! Pop! Pop! Pop! Pop! . . .

Molasses jumped to the floor and fired back.

Blop! Blop! Blop! Blop! . . .

Charlie finally unleashed with the assault weapon.

Tat-tat-tat-tat-tat-tat-tat-tat . . .

Bullets were suddenly flying everywhere, ripping shit
apart. Charlie struggled to maintain his grip as he continued recklessly firing the assault weapon.

Tat-tat-tat-tat-tat-tat-tat . . .

In the wild shoot-out, Kirk pulled out his own gun and
fired several shots in Molasses's direction.

Pop! Pop! Pop!

His shots were close, but not close enough. Kirk was
only using his gunshots for cover to slip out the back door
to safety.

After he made his exit, Molasses turned his attention to
the other men in the room who were firing on him and his
partner.

Pop! Pop! Pop! Pop! . . .

Blauuww! Blauuww! Blauuww! . . .

Pop! Pop! Pop! . . .

There were too many of them for a single gun, no matter
how powerful it was. So Molasses was forced to grab Charlie and help him to use the assault weapon correctly.

Tat-tat-tat-tat-tat-tat-tat-tat-tat . . .

They took out three more men, and the last three were
smart enough to scatter out of there.

Molasses ran to the back door in search of Kirk, but he
was long gone.

"Shit!" Molasses cursed. He knew he had made the
wrong enemy to keep alive. Kirk might not be the man to
commit a murder himself, but he surely had enough people

on his side who would. But if he was dead, he wouldn't be able to talk many folks into his defense.

Charlie joined Molasses outside the back door and began to hurl. The experience had all been a bit much for his stomach to take.

"Too much excitement for you, huh, Charlie?" Molasses teased him.

Charlie didn't answer. He continued to hurl.

LATER that night, Molasses sat with Charlie inside the dark sedan at a new meeting place. The old one was too hot for them now, and off-limits for their safety.

Molasses said, "You know the great thing about this business, Charlie? We kill a lot of people who society don't give a fuck about. They just think of it as another gang war, a fight over drug turf, or some badass finally gettin' his due. Killer . . . unknown."

Molasses chuckled at the idea, like a pure madman. Charlie said nothing. He was actually trying to figure out his moral standing in the whole bloody business. It was a different dilemma to be on the actual killing side of the business instead of acting as the setup man. But murder was murder, and the whole mess of it ran through his mind.

Molasses continued with his musings:

"I want you to keep looking out for whoever put that hit on me, too, Charlie. You hear me? Do an online search or whatever."

Charlie looked at him in confusion.

"You mean, you don't think it was Kirk and his guys?"

Molasses shook his head.

"Naw, it wasn't Kirk."

Charlie suddenly became irate. He was pissed at the idea! All of that for nothing. Molasses was really losing it.

Charlie said, "Well, what the hell did we just do that for? Because you don't like the guy's fuckin' name."

Molasses was more thoughtful about it.

He said, "I just had an urge to fuck with him. If somebody fucks with me, I'm gonna fuck with somebody else. It's 'Molasses's Law,' " he stated.

Charlie said, "Oh, great, that makes a lot of sense. And then you go and involve *me* in it. Now Kirk and his guys can come after me. That was smart."

Molasses told him, "Because you're not invincible, Charlie. That's why I did it. That sideline shit of yours is too sweet of a deal. So I had to let you see what it feels like to be out there in the middle of the action."

Charlie said, "Hell, you're still the main player. *You* make all the big money. I drive all around the country to set things up for you, and I only get ten percent. That's not fair," he informed his partner.

Charlie had been wanting to get that piece of information off his chest for a while.

Molasses only smiled at him. It had been a much sweeter deal for him.

He said, "You want a larger percentage, Charlie? Is that it?"

"That would be nice," his partner answered. "Especially if you plan on putting me in that kind of danger. I thought we had a straight business agreement."

Molasses unexpectedly tossed his arm around Charlie's shoulder inside the sedan.

Charlie responded nervously for a second before he relaxed.

Molasses told him, "We *do* have a business agreement. And you still owe me one from that shit in Texas. But after you square that away, I'll cut you a better deal. All right, Charlie?

"But first things first," he added. "I want to know who tried to kill me."

Charlie calmed down and nodded.

"All right. I'll see what I can find out."

Molasses nodded back to him.

"Good. You go do that for me."

Charlie climbed out of the car and walked off toward his own dark sedan.

Molasses started up the car and drove off into the night. And as he drove through the Chicago streets, he reminisced on his childhood, a childhood that had been largely absent of peace of mind.

Molasses drove down familiar streets in his old neighborhood, where he envisioned things as if they were still happening to him. In vibrant flashbacks he saw himself as a kid, running through the streets of West Side Chicago. He was then joined by Otis, his main boy. They both looked grown beyond their years, with hardened eyes and tough-guy postures. They were manchilds, with missing-in-action fathers and young mothers who were too inexperienced to handle their budding manhood. And as the urban black boys of their tough Chicago home grew old, they learned to pass on their unexplainable pains to those who were weak, or those who were despised as enemies and rival crews.

Molasses saw himself in those rugged streets, growing old again, only to engage in more fistfights while experimenting with the get-high to lose himself in the mad, mad world that he had somehow inherited with his friends and extended family. And he saw himself again with Otis, running frantically from the hungry, flesh-eating bullets that struck Otis in the back, leaving him crying and praying in vain as the life of his best friend slipped away.

That was when Molasses decided there was no God in the ghetto. There was only the devil. Only the devil had power in the streets. And only the devil could make things right. With fire. And with brimstone.

One thing's for sure ... Molasses is one bold motherfucker. He says and does whatever the hell he wants to. And I actually had the nerve to admire him for it.

At a South Side Chicago hairdresser, Molasses's old fling, Pamela Riggs, made a pressing call from her cell phone. She was next up to get her expensive hairdo, but she appeared a bit nervous that day.

"Hello. Yeah. I'm thinking about leaving town for a while. Something just came up," she commented over the line.

Molasses strolled into the shop unexpectedly and caught Pamela's eye. She was still in the middle of her phone call, but after she spotted Molasses in his dark suit and silk tie she quickly ended the call.

"I'll call you back in a few," she said into the cell phone.

She disconnected the call and looked at Molasses in shock. He was still alive, and he had caught up to her before she could leave town. He didn't look too friendly with his noticeable nicks and scars either.

Molasses spoke real smoothly to her.

"You don't look like you're happy to see me. Don't mind these injuries. I had a little accident out on the street the other night."

Pamela was speechless. Her eyes began to search his

well-tailored body for the bulge of his gun. She knew he had one on him. And he did.

Molasses told her, "Let's take a walk outside and talk."

Pamela was defiant in her response to him.

"No."

Molasses eyed her with no time for playfulness. Someone had tried to kill him, and he had his information together now. In fact, Pamela's nervousness only confirmed what Molasses already knew.

He said, "Don't make me repeat myself."

She began to look around the crowded hair salon. Numbers meant safety. Molasses wouldn't dare kill her in front of twelve other people.

However, he was unnerved by the witnesses.

He said, "You know what, I don't care about nobody in here. Now try my patience. *Please.*"

Pamela thought fast and all but told on herself.

"I thought you said you don't do that to women," she reminded him.

He said, "I don't. But we still need to talk."

Pamela remained hesitant, but what other choice did she have? The man wasn't budging until she spoke to him in private. And she realized that aggravating him was probably not a good idea.

She responded to him meekly, "Okay."

But she made sure she left her expensive pocketbook in her chair before she walked out with him. She left it as a reminder to the other women inside the shop that she expected to return shortly.

Outside the shop, Molasses wasted no time with his questions.

"So, who did you tell about my business?" he asked her. "I won't kill you, but I *will* kill them. It's either your life or theirs," he told her bluntly.

Pamela was wide-eyed with panic.

"So you *would* kill me?" she asked him.

Molasses said, "I think you know that already, Pam. And under extreme circumstances like this one, *all* of my rules are breakable. So make sure you tell me what I need to know."

Pamela calmed herself to speak. At least he was being civil with her.

She said, "I didn't tell anyone about your business. I wouldn't do that. I was just frustrated with you, Moe. I mean, you made me feel like . . . trash. You just threw me away. And all I wanted to know is why."

She made it seem as if her explanation would make her actions acceptable to him.

Molasses nodded to her, but he wasn't there for a dispute. Nor was he there to forgive her.

He said, "So, you *did* pay to have me killed, and using my own networks at that."

Charlie had done the research on it and had pointed him in her direction. It was Molasses's fault for allowing Pamela to wander far too close to their game.

Now that Pamela had been busted, she could see that Molasses wasn't planning on letting her ass off the hook. What killer would?

She said, "I'm sorry, Moe. I mean, I just—"

Molasses cut her off.

"You just miss me that damn much, huh?" He finally loosened up and chuckled at his own sarcastic humor.

"I'm actually flattered by it," he told her. "You missed my thing so much that you wanted to kill me for it. That's a hell of a compliment. So how much was I worth to you?"

She refused to go there. It was bad enough that he knew she had ordered the hit.

Molasses was thin on patience. He needed all of his questions answered immediately, before he lost his cool.

"I'm not gonna ask you again," he told her.

She blurted out, "Ten thousand dollars."

Molasses heard that weak-ass amount and frowned. He would have rather been told that he was worth a million dollars. Ten grand wasn't shit to him.

Pamela explained, "That was all I had."

And it was bullshit! Pamela Riggs came from a wealthy Michigan family, and she had access to much more than ten grand.

Molasses figured she was playing his life cheap, like a rich woman would with a man from the streets. He despised that in her the most. He was no more than a toy to her. How ironic was that, considering how he treated his women?

But he was not there to dispute any of that. It was too late for arguments. He was there to set her ass up. He just had to make sure it was her. Killing a woman was still something he had never had to do. Women had been loyal to him, loyal to a fault.

He asked her, "You paid them off already?"

He was solidifying her confession.

Pamela looked at him pleading for mercy. Would he *please* allow her to live?

"Half of it," she answered.

He nodded to her and remained amazingly calm. After all, no one knew what he was there to see her about. Pamela may have been a spoiled woman, but she was still private. She at least had that much on her side.

So Molasses told her, "Here's what I want you to do. You go back in there, get your hair done, look nice and all that, and then you go home and pack up your shit and leave Chicago. You understand me?"

Pamela nodded to him, eagerly.

"Yes," she answered.

He told her, "I don't want to see your face ever again. And if I find out that you told somebody something . . ." He paused for effect. "I'm gonna find you. Believe that."

Pamela insisted, "I didn't tell anyone."

Molasses held up a hand to silence her. He didn't want to hear any more about it.

He said, "All right then. It's done. I'll see you in the afterworld."

Pamela hesitated a second before she walked back into the hair salon. Would he really let her live? She was ready to thank him in the sincere hope that he would.

But Molasses turned his back to her and walked off toward his Navigator, parked up the street from them. He climbed in and took a deep breath. He looked relieved. But at the same time, he looked troubled. Even a coldhearted killer thought about the toil of his work sometimes. Nevertheless, he had to do what he had to do. Killing was how he lived his life. And compromises became fatal.

BEFORE Molasses could pull away from the curb in his Navigator, Janeia Goode popped up at his passenger-side door and tapped on the window. She was wearing a colorful knit hat with a forward brim, and her hair out the sides.

"Shit!" Molasses cursed. She had caught him off guard. He was already reaching for the gun inside his suit jacket.

Janeia was the last person he expected to see. But hell, he *was* on the South Side. She lived there. He just had a lot more pressing matters on his mind.

He rolled down the window to be cordial to her and to ask a few questions.

"How long you been out here?" he asked her. He didn't even bother to say hi. He only wanted to know if she had seen him talking to Pamela in front of the hair salon.

Janeia told him, "I just walked around the corner, actually." Then she looked into his face and became concerned.

"Oh, my God! What happened to you?"

His injuries were not as bad as when he had first received them, but they were still noticeable. And Janeia hadn't seen him up close in weeks.

Molasses took a breath and decided to get her away from there. Either that, or he would have to give her a fast shoulder. So he decided to use a little bit of tact and sugar instead.

"Get in," he told her.

Janeia climbed into the high-seated Navigator as soon as he unlocked the door.

When they drove off down the street, he decided to tell her about his injuries.

"To make a long story short, somebody tried to kill me last week," he told her. "And they crashed and shot up the Bentley. So I've been out here working overtime to find out who it was."

Janeia just stared at him. She figured his dangerous line of work would put him in harm's way sooner or later. What all could she say about it?

She opened her mouth and said, "I'm still here for you. I just want you to know that. Even if you need somebody to help you."

Molasses heard that and began to smile. Janeia was a real piece of work.

He looked into her pleading eyes and asked her, "Can you shoot a gun at my enemies?"

He was only testing her, to see how far she would go with it.

But Janeia never flinched.

She answered, "If that's what you need me to do. All you have to do is tell me who to shoot."

Molasses broke out laughing. Either this chick was crazy, or she was just . . . *crazy*. He couldn't figure her out. Was she bullshitting or what?

He said, "Seriously, I got a lot of loose ends to tie up. So I may need to call you after everything is said and done. Okay?"

She blew him off and said, "You wouldn't need my help then, if everything is said and done."

He nodded to her.

He responded, "No, I don't need it. Not for killing people."

"What do you need me for then?" she asked him.

Molasses was stuck for a minute.

He finally said, "I just need you to keep caring for me like you do."

"Not lately," she responded.

He eyed her and asked, "What do you mean?"

But he knew what the hell she meant. He wasn't spending any more time with her hot ass, and she was *desperate* for him.

So she went ahead and explained it to him.

"I mean, you haven't been calling me or seeing me or anything. So what do you need me to do? Do you remember what I needed from you?"

Molasses didn't like her tone anymore. And after just dealing with Pamela's problem, he finally realized that Charlie may have been right; he needed to leave the women alone for a while. They simply needed more than he could give them. And he had other shit to do. He wasn't a damn caretaker for their emotional needs. Save that shit!

So he said, "You know what, let me call you later on before I get upset in here."

He was already pulling over to the curb to let her frustrated ass out.

Janeia looked away from him and didn't say a word. It was that time again, when a nigga she loved started acting up. And she was tired of that shit.

She said, "So, I guess I have to walk back now."

Molasses took a deep breath and stopped at the curb. He had to use more of his intelligence. Ice didn't work well with women. More than anything, women responded to opportunity, an opportunity for love. So he gave that to her, a fucking Hallmark card in a colorful envelope to set up on her mind.

He looked into her eyes with subtlety and said, "Janeia . . . I will call you tonight. Okay? But right now"—he shook his head—"I just need to handle what I need to handle. You understand that? Look at me."

Janeia looked at the card, read it, and accepted it, just like he knew she would. She had no other choice.

So she nodded and said, "All right. I'm sorry." Then she climbed out of the Navigator on faith.

As soon as Janeia watched Molasses drive off, she grumbled, "Okay, we're gonna see about that shit tonight. If he wants to play games, I can play games, too."

She didn't go for the Hallmark card shit. She only allowed Molasses to *think* she did. She had too much ammunition already. She saw him dealing with the same girl from the restaurant. She saw him kiss another in his car. And she had found out about a few more of his bitches by asking the right people about him. He just didn't know who *she* knew. And he definitely didn't know what she was capable of.

"Oh, we'll see," she continued to grumble as she walked back toward the hair salon.

Whuurrp! Whuurrp!

She turned and spotted a black cop in his police cruiser. She hadn't done anything wrong, nor did she recognize him as a friend, so she ignored him.

The black cop set off his siren again and pulled up to the curb in front of her.

Whuurrp! Whuurrp!

He rolled down his window to talk to her.

Janeia stopped, irritated by it.

"Is there a problem?" she asked the officer. She was already on edge.

He said, "I just needed to ask you a few questions about Warren Hamilton, or better known as Molasses."

He watched her carefully to see how she would respond.

Janeia thought faster than the officer expected. There was no sense in denying that she knew the man. She suspected that the cop already knew something. Why else would he approach her about it? He probably even witnessed her climbing out of the Navigator. So she decided to use what he knew to her own advantage.

"What about him?"

She planned to ask the cop as many questions as he would ask her.

However, the officer changed the approach on her.

He asked her, "Do you love him?"

Janeia paused. She then looked closely at his badge. It read "L. Barrett."

"Haven't I seen you around before?" she asked him. She decided to change her approach as well. What was the cop really after?

He said, "Yeah, you've seen me before. I was around when your boyfriend picked you up in his Bentley. You know it got shot up recently, right?"

Janeia paused for a minute.

"What do you know about it?" she asked him.

"I'm trying to find out what *you* know," he told her. "But I will tell you this, I wouldn't be surprised if a woman had something to do with it. You know what I mean? He seems to know a whole lot of women. But the guys . . . they all seem to be scared of him. Not the ones who tried to kill him, but you know what I mean. This guy seems to be real *intimidating* to some people."

He smiled at Janeia and asked her, "So how do you feel about, you know, Molasses having all these other women? Are you into that sharing-a-man thing?"

He seemed more interested in irritating her than in getting any real answers. So she started walking again. She didn't have time for that.

"You don't want to talk about your boyfriend anymore?" the officer asked her as she left. "I'm just trying to figure out what's so attractive about him, that's all."

Janeia ignored him. Obviously, the officer realized Molasses wasn't too keen on keeping an organized stable. And he didn't get a chance to talk to the girl as long as he wanted to; however, he did manage to keep her from snooping around Pamela Riggs at the hair salon. Janeia was too hyper now to remain civil, and she didn't want to haul off and hurt the woman behind the wrong attitude. So she decided to return home instead, to plot out her next move, while waiting to see if Molasses would actually call her, like he said he would.

OFFICER Barrett smiled to himself as the flustered college girl walked away from his squad car. He had done some research on her as well. He figured it was only good for a Chicago State student to rethink her relationship with a man like Molasses. Maybe she didn't know the lifestyle he lived after dark. Or maybe she *did* know. Nevertheless, he believed that she was still a good girl who would make the right decision if given enough information. He was just optimistic about her choices, and he wanted to make sure that she had them available before she slid too far down the wrong road with the man.

THAT night, outside her five-story apartment building near downtown Chicago, Pamela Riggs shoved her last bag into the backseat of her champagne-colored Lexus and shut the door. She then hopped in behind the wheel to hit the road. She looked damned good, too, in a brown suede skirt, a tight knit top, and black stilettos; her hair shoulder-length and newly curled.

She drove down her street and made it to the first corner stop sign before a masked and gloved man sprinted up to her driver's-side window with a gun out.

"Give me this fucking car!" he screamed at her.

Pamela was defiant again.

She yelled, "Shit! Look, I'm on my way out the city. This is the wrong night for this shit. Carjack somebody the hell else. Can't you see all of the luggage I have in here?

"It's too much evidence," she told him. "So go 'jack a damn empty car."

That was Pamela's way, a spoiled woman who was used to giving people orders and having them obey her.

But the masked man wasn't hearing it.

"Get out of the car before I have to kill you," he warned her. His long, black gun was right in her face, and a decision had to be made fast.

Pamela was ready to either break down and cry, or try to run that motherfucker over. But instead, she did what he said and climbed out of the car for him to take it.

"Shit!" she cursed again. She had not taken her more expensive things anyway. She planned on having a moving company do the job once she had settled in a new place somewhere in Missouri. She wasn't going back home to Michigan, either.

But once she stepped out of the car with her one carrying bag of money, credit cards, and identification, the masked man reached out and snatched it from her.

Pamela was shocked.

"What the hell are you doing?" she screamed at him again.

She thought he just wanted the damn car. But then he shot her in the stomach with a silencer.

Theessrrpp!

"Unnhh!" Pamela moaned with her eyes wide open. She thought about the whole setup and mumbled "Molasses" as she crumpled to the ground, whimpering in pain.

The masked man shook a bit with the gun in his hand before he shot her again in the chest.

Theessrrpp!

He then jumped inside of the Lexus and sped off before the next few cars had reached the intersection.

AT their new meeting place, Molasses and Charlie sat inside another dark sedan. Out of the blue, Charlie rushed to push open the passenger-side door so he could hurl onto the ground.

Molasses watched him and grinned.

When Charlie recovered and wiped his mouth with his clothes, he asked his partner, "So, we're even now, right?"

Molasses nodded to him.

"Yeah."

Charlie mumbled, "Good. Because I don't want to ever have to do that again."

He hesitated before he continued.

"She said your name before she died," he commented.

Molasses looked concerned. He didn't expect to hear that. "She did?"

Charlie told him, "Yeah. So I had to shoot her again."

"Where did you shoot her the first time?"

"I think in her stomach."

Molasses frowned at him and shook his head.

He said, "Yeah, I gotta get you back behind the computer. You don't know what the hell you're doing out here."

"I tried to explain that to you already," Charlie reminded him.

"Yeah, yeah, I know," Molasses grumbled. "So, how does seventy-five/twenty-five sound to you?"

"Not as good as forty/sixty," Charlie responded.

Molasses looked at his partner and chuckled at him as if he was only joking.

"Get the fuck out of here," he told him.

Charlie smiled back at him.

He said, "I figured I would at least *ask.*"

Molasses told him, "We'll do seventy/thirty and call it a day."

Charlie nodded to him.

"I guess that's fair enough for now. Since you did pay me for this job."

"All up front, too," Molasses reminded him. "Now that's looking out."

He then decided to move on to their next item of business.

"So you have an address for this guy in Indiana?"

Charlie pulled out another one of his handy printouts.

"Yeah."

"Well, let me go take care of that while it's still fresh on my mind," Molasses said of the new job. "I need a break from Chicago for a while anyway. I might even head to Ohio for a week or so after this one."

"What about Kirk?" Charlie asked him. "He's still out there now."

Molasses shook his head.

"Don't worry about him. He's old-school. He knows the rules. We'll have us another day to dance in the future. But not while shit is still hot. It would point too many fingers in his direction now. But do look out for him," Molasses warned.

"Oh, you don't have to tell me that. He knows what I look like," Charlie responded.

He said, "And since we're on the subject of rules, and everything, I think you need to add some new ones yourself."

Molasses was intrigued by the idea.

"Oh, yeah? Like what?"

Charlie said, "Rule number six: Never underestimate the vengeance of a woman. Especially when she has it bad for you."

Molasses laughed it off. He said, "Yeah, I was just thinking about that earlier today. These women can be vicious."

Charlie continued:

"And rule number seven: Stay low-key, like I do."

Molasses said, "You mean dress and drive like a square? I don't think I can do that, Charlie."

Charlie shook his head and hesitated. Nevertheless, he had to state what was on his mind at the moment.

He said, "To tell you the truth, Moe, you needed to get rid of that car a long time ago. It just brought too much attention. And you need to buy a nice place out in the suburbs somewhere and get away from the trappings of the city."

Molasses just smiled at him.

"In other words, I should try to go legit, huh? And put my money in stocks and bonds and shit?"

Charlie answered, "Exactly. What do you think I plan on doing?" He said, "I mean, we have to think about the real value here, Moe. Collect a real living and get out while you can and into a much less lethal business. And move the hell away from Chicago where we have too many enemies now."

Molasses was enjoying the conversation. Charlie gave him a lot to think about. Then again, most men *would* think a lot more after escaping death.

He asked his partner, "You got any other new rules for me, Charlie?"

Charlie answered, "Well, this one's an old one." Then he paused again. He said, "For the last time, Moe, leave your women *out* of our business. I mean, I'm not telling you not to get laid or anything, I'm just saying to get laid on your *free time* and not while you're on a job. And *please* stop telling them what you do. I mean, you're the *best*, man, you really are, but . . ."

Charlie stopped and shook his head. He just hoped and prayed that his lady-loving partner got the point.

Molasses said, "Charlie, you're trying mighty hard to turn me into a damn square, man. I mean, do I seem like a newspaper-on-the-front-lawn type to you?" he questioned.

Charlie answered, "Well, just look at it this way, squares live longer, and they spend a lot less time in jail."

Molasses eyed him and said, "So, why are you hanging out and killing people with me then, Charlie, since you admire the square life so much?"

Charlie smiled and said, "I'm just trying to make enough money out here to *afford* to be a square again."

Molasses looked at him and laughed.

He said, "You a white boy, all right. Money talks . . . and everything else you say is just bullshit."

THAT same night, Janeia Goode sat in her kitchen and sipped orange juice from a tall glass. She was dressed in a long, drab nightshirt with nowhere to go and no one to be with. But her mother walked into the kitchen dressed to impress for the night. She wore a jazzy dark green two-piece with a new, curly-top hairdo. She was all spunky, energetic, and ready for her hot date.

She noticed her daughter's glum mood at the table and commented on it.

She said, "You haven't been so happy around here lately, Janeia." She grinned and added, "Your new boyfriend act-

ing up? You better call Rasheed before that boy gets married to some groupie out in California somewhere."

Janeia didn't respond to her. It seemed as if she was in a
daze.

She asked her mother in a dry monotone, "Where are
you going tonight?"

Her mother looked at her as if she was crazy.

She said, "I ain't dead yet. I'm going *out*. I'm gonna go
and get my groove on."

She grabbed her purse and keys and headed for the front
door, leaving her daughter home by herself.

Janeia looked depressed, as if life had been sucked out of
her. Love was a real motherfucker when it didn't work.
Molasses had really turned her out. Or maybe she had
turned herself out by believing in him so much. Like his
phone call. It was only more game to gas up her head.

Maybe he had gone back to the woman at the hair salon,
or the bitch he had kissed in his car that night. Or another
bitch. Or another bitch. They were *all* bitches to Janeia.
They were just getting in her way. *Bitches!*

Janeia looked down at a large black pocketbook that sat
between her legs on the floor. She had gotten herself a gun,
a blond wig, and some sunglasses to get away with her own
killings if she had to. She had some underground friends
herself. And she knew where she could get some things.

Killing people seemed to work pretty good for Molasses.
But Janeia was not interested in money. She just wanted the
respect. Killing folks got people's undivided attention. It
did for him. They were *all* afraid of Molasses. And maybe
she'd make a few people afraid of *her* now.

When the kitchen telephone rang, Janeia answered it
with all the hope in the world, praying that it would be Mr.
Warren Hamilton. Only his love could save her from her
thoughts of madness. It was all because of him anyway. Or

them, all the bad men who had scorned her in her past relationships. And maybe Molasses was the final straw.

"Hello," she answered.

"Janeia, what the hell is going on? You don't talk to me no more. You don't call me. We don't do lunch at school together. You're hardly even there anymore. I mean, what is the damn problem?"

It was Brenda, and she was letting her girl have it.

She said, "This love jones shit *seriously* has to stop with you. Don't let this guy destroy our friendship and everything else you need to do. What is wrong with you?"

It was too late for reason. Janeia was out there already. She was lost somewhere in her own world. She sat at the kitchen table and twisted her hair with her fingers. Another man had left her wet, horny, begging, and out to dry.

He loves me. He loves me not. He loves me. He loves me not . . .

But she was still willing to protect him.

"You don't tell people about him, do you?" she asked Brenda. "Because you really shouldn't. That's *our* business. Mine and his."

Over at her apartment, Brenda stopped pacing the room like an angry mother hen and just stared at the phone.

She said, "What? What am I gonna tell people about him, Janeia? You haven't told me a damn thing about this man," she reminded her friend. "All I know is that he's into some deep shit that you won't even talk about. Dollar Bill won't even talk about him. And you *know* how much he likes to run *his* mouth."

"Well, stop worrying about it!" Janeia snapped over the line. "His life is none of your damn business anyway."

Brenda was surprised and hurt by her friend's outrage.

She said, "Oh, it's like *that*, is it? I'm only trying to look out for you. I don't really care about him, to be honest about it."

Janeia was incensed. She stood up from her seat at the kitchen table and hollered into the phone.

"Nobody fuckin' *asked* you to care about him! You don't even *know* him! But I *do*! Okay?"

She even felt an urge to hang up the phone on her girl. And she did. The chick was straight tripping.

She strutted around the kitchen table and included Brenda on her hit list.

"Fuckin' bitch. She don't know shit. She never had a man. That's why she's always sweatin' my guys."

BRENDA held the phone in her hand and looked at it in disbelief. "I can't believe this. She has really gon' overboard this time."

ON Janeia's end, she got her beef with Brenda all out of her system, and then calmly sat back down to begin plotting on Molasses. She would defend the man on one hand, but on the other, she wanted to kill him. Didn't she tell him that she would love him no matter what? Didn't she accept his lifestyle without judgment? And didn't she tell his ass never to leave her? But there she was, lonely as hell again with not even a phone call from him.

ONE thing was for sure, there was a lot going on that night. Molasses even stopped by to visit his mother, of all people. She let him into the house dressed in black satin pajamas and wasted no time telling him what she thought about his life. Warren wasn't getting any younger, and she still didn't have any grandkids yet.

She said, "Warren, I think it's about time I told you this, but I think you need to settle down with a good woman. You know, just to keep you home more and out of trouble," she told him.

"You're all that I got in this world, baby, and I'm beginning to get concerned about you."

He hadn't even gotten a chance to sit down yet.

He smiled at his mother and asked her, "Is that right?"

Even Mom was looking to lock him down.

She told him, "It's for your own good, baby."

Molasses nodded. He said, "All right, well . . . I'll think about it."

His mother rarely asked him about the particulars of his life. So he assumed that she didn't want to know. And she didn't. Not knowing allowed her to rest easier. She just figured that a woman and family would make him think twice about taking too many chances.

"I'm serious about this, Warren," she pleaded with him.

"All right, I hear you. I love you, too," he added for sarcasm.

His mother stopped and stared at him as he eased down into the black leather sofa. She was really concerned about him now. It was no damn joke.

She said, "You know what, I look at this recent incident as a test. Now you have a real chance to live a good life, Warren. But it's up to you to go ahead and take that chance. And as much as you may not want to hear it, I would rather have you settle down with a woman and stick around than to lose you while you're still running around doing God knows what in these streets."

Molasses responded, "Well, these streets . . ." and he stopped himself. His mother didn't want to know where his money came from. And whether she asked him for it, took it from him, and spent plenty of it didn't matter. The truth was the truth. His way of life was a long walk on thin ice. No matter how good he was as a killer, he couldn't argue with that reality.

Ms. Hamilton walked out of the room without another word to her son. She had said enough, and he was a grown-ass man who would live or die with his own decisions.

...

WHILE he rested at his mother's house, Molasses began to think about his fetish for fine women who loved bad boys. Was it his fault they made the decisions they made? Of course not. They were all grown women. He had been honest with all of them. And he had made promises to none of them. So he figured he owed them nothing.

Nevertheless, if they believed he owed them something, then their perceptions became their realities, which had led one woman to lose her life over him.

"Yeah," Molasses mumbled to himself, "I need to chill for a while."

Just as he made his decision, the cell phone on his hip went off. He looked down and read the number. It was Annette. He wondered immediately if she had heard about him murdering her old boyfriend. He decided to answer it just to find out.

"Yeah, what's up?" he asked her.

He sounded cold and distant. It was all her move.

She said, "Hey, what are you doing tonight?"

"I'm just sitting here relaxing," he told her.

It was close to midnight.

She said, "You feel like seeing me?"

Molasses paused. Would he bring up a conversation about her old boyfriend, or would she? Did she even know about it? Maybe she did, maybe she didn't. But Kirk knew about her. And he knew that Molasses had taken her. So all bets were off. Molasses couldn't trust the girl. There were too many questions to ask and answers to know. So he decided to take the safe route.

He breathed over the line and said, "You know, I'm a little tired tonight. I think I might have to pass on this one."

She asked him, "Are you sure? I mean, I got plenty of energy tonight, and if you're tired, all you have to do is lay

back and relax . . . and I'll make sure you feel comfortable."
Then she chuckled at it, like a telephone sex freak.

It would have sounded inviting on another day and from
another woman, but not tonight, and not from Annette. He
just couldn't afford to trust the bitch. She was too deep into
the street game. Molasses needed a woman who was not in
the game at all, an innocent girl.

So even while he held Annette on the line, he began to
think of Janeia, his dedicated college chick.

"So, what are you thinking?" Annette pressed him.

"Ah . . . naw, I'ma have to take a rain check, baby girl.
I'm just a li'l too tired right now. But can you do me a
favor?" he asked her.

"Yeah, what's that?"

"Can you keep it wrapped tight for me?"

She laughed and said, "I'll see what I can do. But I might
have to play with it a little bit. It's lonely."

He laughed back to her.

He said, "As long as you don't give it away to another
soldier, I'm cool. Do what you gotta do. I'm just sorry I
can't be there to watch you."

"You can be here. That's all on you," she told him.

He said, "Yeah, I know, but just save it for me. All right?
Can you do that?"

She said, "You gon' do the same for me?"

"Do what?" he asked her. But he knew what the hell she
was talking about. He just liked to hear the confessions.

She said, "Save mine from the other cheerleaders out
there."

Molasses laughed out loud. He didn't realize Annette
had that kind of game with her. And maybe she didn't.
Maybe she was just trying to set his ass up. Game recognize
game. So he put her slick ass on ice.

He told her, "I'll think about it and call you back with my answer." And he hung up before she could argue.

The girl had gotten to him, though. Women were fun to deal with. He had to admit that. No wonder he liked fucking with them so much. But the karma was right. He needed to deal with more virginal chicks for better results and protection. Chicks who had no idea how he made his living.

He thought about Janeia Goode again and froze. She was a good girl, a young, developing college chick. But he had already ruined her by exposing her to his lifestyle. And now she was ready to live it with him. Was that a good thing, or a bad thing?

He needed more time to figure that out. But how much more time did he have with her? She was already pressed about him. She was even running out in the middle of the street after his ass.

Molasses thought about that and chuckled.

"Yeah, that girl in love for real," he told himself.

But he wasn't ready to talk to her yet. He needed his mind to be right before he called her. He was still shifty at the moment, and a shifty mind would make him sound weak. He had that much respect for the girl. Her love game was stronger than most. So she would just have to wait until he was ready to deal with her.

Then again, he had met this new square chick a few weeks back who lived on the North Side. She was eager and innocent, too, and just out of college. So he thought about giving her a call, just to try out how different things could be on the square side of town.

Molasses punched up her name and number and called her immediately. But as soon as her line began to ring, he thought again about the time. Was it too late for her? It was a Thursday night. She probably had to work in the morning.

"Hello," she answered. It was too late to stop the phone call—she had already answered. And it sounded like she was at a party.

"You at a party?" Molasses asked her. He could hear the music and club noise in the background.

"Yeah, who is this?" she asked him.

"It's Molasses. You don't remember me?"

She heard his name and changed her tone immediately.

"Oh, yeah, hi. I didn't think you would call me."

He smiled before he responded to her. She even sounded like a damn square. She was all excited and shit.

He said, "Why not? I asked you for your number, didn't I?" He was real cool about it.

She said, "Yeah, but you now, you were all high-balling in your Bentley and stuff. Maybe you just wanted to see if you could get it."

He said, "Yeah, well, I got it, and I'm using it now."

"Good. Use it all you want to," she told him.

He said, "I don't have that Bentley no more."

He wanted to shut her big eyes as quickly as possible. Charlie was right. That Bentley drew a lot of attention.

She asked him, "Why, what happened to it? You traded it in? Was it a rental?"

"Naw, it wasn't no rental. But some drunk asshole crashed into it last week. Fucked me all up, too."

"Oh, my God!" she said. "Are you all right?"

He grinned his ass off and said, "Yeah, I'm all right. I gotta few nicks and bruises and shit, but I'm still a good-looking nigga."

"I don't doubt it," she told him.

He said, "Well, this party must be boring if you're over there talking to me. It sounds like you're ready to leave."

The motherfucker couldn't help himself. Strong game just poured out of his body.

The chick chuckled and said, "Yeah, it's just a poetry set downtown. I'm ready to leave as soon as my girlfriends are."

"And what if they're not ready to leave?"

She said, "Well . . ."

It was up to him. What did he have in mind?

Again, Molasses couldn't help it. The shit was just that easy to him.

He said, "Well, what time do I need to get you back to your girlfriends?"

The square chick broke down and laughed. Then she got serious.

"Excuse me? I don't roll like that. My friends are not in authority here."

"It that a fact?"

"Yes, that's a fact."

Molasses paused. He needed to evaluate if he was still tired, because this square chick was ready for the taking.

He said, "So you're right downtown?"

"On Michigan Avenue."

There was an awkward silence between them. She was waiting for him to make his move. If Molasses hadn't been thinking earlier about giving his women a break for a while, he would have already made it. But fuck it! He decided to go for broke anyway. He was a man with an appetite.

He asked her, "You ever tried the late-night wine at the Maximum Hotel?"

She chuckled again. She said, "Actually, I've never been there. But it looks nice."

That was all Molasses needed to hear.

*It's amazing how much you can
accomplish when you have the time and
the willpower to do it. . . . I even surprise
myself sometimes.*

Janeia continued to stare at the telephone in her kitchen as if
her life depended on it. And it did, because she felt as if she
would die without Molasses. He had gotten inside of her
bloodstream to become the oxygen in her veins. Without
him, the strung-out chick found it hard to breathe. And when
she received no phone call from him that night, she stood up
from the kitchen table and grabbed her large black pocketbook from the floor, a time bomb awaiting detonation.

BACK out on Chicago's streets, Molasses's Navigator traveled rapidly toward downtown. From out of the dark, red,
white, and blue police lights suddenly flashed from behind
him.

With no other vehicle in proximity, Molasses knew the
police cruiser could only be after him. And he was pissed as
he pulled over.

"What the fuck is this?!"

Officer Barrett popped up at his driver's-side window
with a flashlight. Molasses rolled it down ready to beef with
whoever, and he was surprised to see him.

Officer Barrett was surprised himself.

"Well, well, well. What happened to the Bentley?" he teased.

Molasses responded to him with a straight face.

"You know, this city is too big for you to keep running into me, man. Are you following me? I think I may need to talk to my lawyer about this."

"Actually, I was on my way in for the night, and I happened to see you miss that last stop sign back there," the officer told him.

He said, "But I didn't know it was you, Warren. You're not the only one driving a black Navigator in Chicago. This is a popular vehicle."

He was only stating a fact.

He said, "I'm surprised myself at how many times I keep bumping into you. Maybe it's divine intervention. So I figure I'll try and help you out before you make the *big* mistake."

Then he smiled and said, "I'll give it to you, you cover up your tracks pretty good. But you'll slip up sooner or later. They always do."

Molasses asked him, "Are you sure about that?"

Officer Barrett stared at him and kept his cool.

"You're not *that* smart, Molasses. None of us are."

Molasses nodded to him.

"Can I go now? Or are you gonna write me another ticket?"

The officer shook his head.

"No, no ticket tonight," he told him. "This will just be a warning on the house."

He asked, "Where are you headed to this time of night anyway?"

"To pick up a date," Molasses told him. He figured the man would leave him alone if he pushed the mack game. All men understood the power of testosterone.

But the officer frowned at him.

He said, "I thought your girlfriend lived back on the South Side."

They were closer to downtown.

Molasses frowned back at him. The officer was now telling on himself.

"What girlfriend? You know something I don't know?" Molasses quizzed him.

He had plenty of women on the South Side. South Side Chicago was *huge*. What girl had the officer seen him with? He hoped and prayed it wasn't Pamela Riggs. Her death was still fresh, and he had just been with her on the South Side that afternoon.

But Officer Barrett hadn't seen him with Pamela. He was referring to Janeia Goode, the Chicago State University student. However, he decided to keep that information to himself. Maybe he had said too much already. So he wanted to cover his tracks to keep the innocent girl from catching hell for his slipup.

"I'll just tell you this, Warren." He waited to have his full attention. "Don't fuck up the lives of good people on account of your bullshit, you hear me? Now if you wanna continue dealing with the slimeballs of society, then be my guest. You'll all get rid of each other sooner or later. But when you cross that line and fuck up the lives of good people. That's when it's gonna be your ass. And I'll make *personally* certain of that," the officer added.

Molasses heard his words loud and clear. There was no further need for comment. They were on opposite sides of the law. What else was a police officer supposed to say?

So Molasses asked him real politely, "May I go now?"

Officer Barrett stared at him and warned him one more time. "Leave the good people alone."

Molasses nodded to him and said nothing about it.

"Have a good night, Officer." And he drove off.

OFFICER Barrett watched the massive SUV pull into the street and head up the block. He then walked back to his police cruiser and climbed in.

He took a deep breath and mumbled, "Some guys just don't deserve the breaks they get." And he vowed to make sure he looked after Janeia's safety. She would be his official project now, just for running his mouth and getting himself involved in her personal business.

MOLASSES drove away from the irritating black cop and realized that he would have to kill the man or leave Chicago for good. He had even given the damn cop one of his fake business cards. How dumb a move was that?

He thought about it all and cursed, "That motherfucker!"

He didn't even feel good about picking up the square chick anymore. He was thinking about getting out of Dodge now. Pamela Riggs's murder had to be reported on the news by then. But Molasses barely watched the news. The news made him nervous. He would rather not know the cops were on his trail. He could act more natural that way. And it had worked for him. But once a criminal knew that the cops were on to his shit, it caused him to overreact.

Molasses considered himself a smooth criminal. He plotted well, and executed carefully. So the cops had to prove the shit. And if they couldn't, they had to let the nigga go. Plain and simple.

So he said, "Fuck that! I'm not running. I got a girl to get." And he continued on his way toward Michigan Avenue.

•••

JANEIA rode a half-empty Chicago bus in a vengeful daze, wearing a long, navy raincoat that covered everything down to her knees. Her hair was pulled back under a matching rain hat. But there was no rain, only a heart broken beyond repair.

She rode the bus and stared out the window at everything. Nothing meant anything without a warm body to hold. And she didn't want to hold just any body.

"Hey, ah . . . you headed anywhere in particular?"

Janeia looked and spotted an old-time player in his forties who had eased up to sit in the seat across from her. He still had his hair slicked to the back with too much perm gel. She didn't even bother to look at the rest of him. He wasn't worth it. So she ignored his ass.

He said, "If you need somebody to talk to, sometimes you can find them in the most awkward places."

He spoke it like a true pimp, all cool, calm, and logical. He was just hollering at the wrong young woman on the wrong late night. The chick was packed, and with a nasty attitude.

She looked at him with the stare of the devil in her eyes and said, "If you need to find a new, young, dumb whore for your stable, you better look somewhere the fuck else." That was all she needed to say.

The old-time player looked over at how tightly she held her big black bag at her side, and he knew that a pretty girl like that wouldn't talk so strongly to him without packing something lethal. So he stood up and walked away to leave her ass the hell alone. There were plenty of nicer young women out there to talk to.

Janeia watched his retreat after her viperous tongue had bit him, and she liked it. Who wouldn't like immediate results? That only made her feel more righteous about what she planned to do. All she needed was the whereabouts.

•••

AT the Maximum Hotel in downtown Chicago, Molasses strutted up to the reception counter with his new chick holding his hand. She was an exotic, Indian-brown bombshell with wavy hair that dropped to her shoulders over a gold silk blouse and a black silk skirt.

Damn he had it good! This square chick was the kind of girl that college boys would blow their whole tuitions on. And Molasses was ready to pull her fine ass with one phone call.

It just didn't seem logical, but the shit happened every night of the week. Fine women loved themselves some abrasive candy.

OUTSIDE the hotel in a parked car sat an eager-to-please hustler. He was on the extraslim, wiry side, in a Chicago White Sox cap and a matching white-on-black jersey. He just couldn't believe his good fortune. So he jumped on his cell phone to spread the good news.

"Hey, I just spotted your boy."

JANEIA damn near dropped her cell phone as she held it to her ear on the bus.

"Where?" she asked her informant.

Women had connections, too. All they had to do was sweet-talk the right guy with a hard-on in his pants.

"At the Maximum Hotel, downtown," the hard-up hustler told her.

Janeia paused and thought about it. She needed more privacy to get more information out of him.

"Hold on, I'll call you right back in a few minutes."

She stood up to get off the bus, with the old-time player watching her every move.

When she climbed down the stairs and stepped off, he mumbled to anyone who was listening, "That's a mean-ass broad right there. She got it *in her.* Somebody did her *wrong.*"

THE eager hustler waited inside his car for Janeia's call-back. He had the ringer on vibrate and it shook his hand when it rang.

"Yeah," he answered.

Janeia told him, "Try and find out what room he's checking into. Is he with somebody?"

"Yeah," he answered. "He's with this *bad* . . ." he caught himself and said, "she not as bad as you, though. She can't deal with you, Janeia."

He wanted to make sure he remained on Janeia's good side.

She blew him off and said, "Yeah, whatever, just find out what room he's in."

"What you gon' do?" he asked her. He wondered how far she was willing to go with her madness.

"Don't worry about it," she told him. "And just forget this whole night ever happened . . . or any other night after this," she added, just in case things didn't go the way she wanted them to the first time. "You hear me?" she asked him.

"Yeah, I got you. This our thing."

Janeia didn't respond to that.

She told him, "So go find everything out and call me back with it. I'm on my way. But don't hang around there for me. I'll do this on my own."

The hustler hung up the phone and shook his head. "This girl crazy," he said out loud.

Nevertheless, he wondered just how crazy she was willing to be. As if it was all a fucking joke. So he climbed out of the car and thought about how he would get the information for her.

•••

INSIDE the enormous hotel room on the fourteenth floor, Molasses poured a tall glass of white wine for his lady friend.

She smiled from the king-size bed. She had kicked off her shoes and curled up her legs.

"I guess I see why they call this place *the maximum*," she commented.

Everything was extralarge: the size of the room, the bathroom, the tall ceilings, the television, and the giant-window view of Chicago.

Molasses grinned at her.

He said, "Yeah, that's how I like it." And he brought her the glass of wine.

She took her first sip and asked him, "So, how did you have this accident again?"

He blew her off. "I don't even wanna talk about that no more. I miss my Bentley already."

"You're not gonna get it fixed?" she quizzed him.

He looked at her fine ass and joined her on the bed.

"Do you know how much it's gonna cost to fix that car? Once they gave me the estimate, I told my insurance people to give me the money so I can put that back in the bank."

She smiled and said, "I know that's right. Those cars are very expensive."

"So are you," he told her.

She stopped and stared at him. She didn't like the sound of that.

"What do you mean by that?"

Molasses looked at this dime-piece broad and could just imagine what she would have a weak motherfucker do for even a sniff of her punany. But he wasn't weak. He was the opposite.

So he looked this chick in the eyes and said, "It takes a whole lot of confidence to fuck with a girl like you. And that's expensive. 'Cause niggas with broke confidence can't afford you. But I happen to be a rich nigga. And I don't need no car to be rich. Real wealth is all about how you play your game in life. You understand me? So let's drink to that. You in good hands now."

He reached out and tapped the chick's glass with his, and he already knew that her panties were wet and ready to be slid to the floor. She confirmed it when she sat there and smiled her cute ass off.

"I see you have a way with women," she commented. It was better to say anything than to sit there feeling stupid. Molasses was overwhelming her. That's what he always did to a woman. So it was best to stay away from his ass. If they could manage to.

Instead of responding to her weak return of his powerful serve, he went ahead and planted a wine-wet kiss on her sexy-ass lips.

Then the chick broke away and got all nervous.

"I think this is all going a little too fast."

Molasses kept his cool. He had been there before. Not every chick will fuck him the first time. So he laid back and relaxed.

He said, "You're right. I gotta learn how to slow down . . . and just enjoy the moment."

He stared up into empty space while sipping his wine. And he thought about Janeia. She had served her game as strongly as he could serve his. He missed her now. She was able to rock him on his heels.

His square chick began to study his demeanor and the seriousness of his injured face.

"What do you do?" she asked him.

It was the golden question. Would he keep her square, or would he pull her over to the dark side?

"I'm trying to decide on that now," he told her.

That left her confused again.

"What?"

She figured he was some kind of high-status business-man. He carried himself like an entertainment manager, a Damon Dash type, who didn't talk as fast.

He told her, "Sometimes you get to a point in your life where you don't know what the hell you want to do tomor-row. You just know you wanna be alive somewhere."

She nodded and caught on to him.

"Yeah, I've felt like that a lot of times," she confessed.

But Molasses didn't have anything else to say about it. He was still thinking about Janeia. Then he got a hard-on, imagining how things would be if she was there with him instead of this extrasquare chick.

"What are you thinking about right now?" she asked him. She could tell that his mind was taking a trip some-where. He didn't seem as focused on her anymore. And she had just asked him the wrong question.

At the moment, he really didn't care about the girl. The charade was over. He wanted Janeia back. He didn't care about the consequences of his brutal honesty either.

He asked the girl, "You really wanna know?"

She thought about it for a minute and said, "Yeah, I do."

So he told her ass the truth.

He said, "I want some pussy right now. And that's all I'm really thinking about."

He didn't care if that pretty bitch jumped out the win-dow and attempted to fly. She asked him what he was think-ing, and he told her. And he didn't feel like explaining shit, either. So he expected her to get all upset, call him a dog, and all that other shit, before she grabbed her things and left. Either that, or she'd respect his game, take off her clothes, and give the man some pussy for being real about it. That's what going for broke was all about.

So Molasses looked her in the eyes and waited for her move.

She said, "Well, why do you have to call it that? I hate that word."

"What else you want me to call it?" he asked her. He waited for an answer.

She stared back at him and began to smile.

She said, "Are you gonna pour me some more wine? I need to be in the mood for that."

He said, "I think you in the mood already. You don't need no more wine. That's a cop-out. Do what your body wants you to do."

He told her, "You too fine for that gettin'-drunk-to-fuck shit. And I wouldn't let you cheat me that way. If you gon' give it up to me, you gon' give it up with your *mind*. Fuck that wine."

The chick broke out laughing. And she was offended by it all. Sure she was. What self-respecting woman wouldn't be? Nevertheless, the nigga talked so strongly to her that she knew she'd be bored as soon as she left the room. So what choice did she have but to give him what he wanted?

She looked down at the bed and couldn't even face him. He had sized her up so well that she was embarrassed.

She said, "You are . . . you are just . . ."

"I'm just what? A *man*?"

She responded "Yeah" and looked into his face.

He said, "And you respect that, right?"

She nodded. "I respect it."

"So what do you want to do then?"

She got all bashful.

"I mean, you want me to say it."

Molasses chuckled and finally let the girl off the hook. "Naw, you don't have to say it. But what you can do is go on over there and turn off the lights, walk back over to the bed, and take them clothes off, and I'll know just what you mean."

Then he waited again for her to make her move.

And sure enough, she grinned at him, stood up from the bed, walked over to turn off the lights, and came back to the bed to strip naked for him. And her shit was wetter than Lake Michigan before he even touched her.

JANEIA arrived at the door of room 1415 at the worst time in the world for a woman. She could hear the strong fucking Molasses was putting on this bitch as clear as day.

"Oooooh, yeeah. Oooooh, yesss."

"This what you needed, right?"

"Yeeeaahh, bay-bee."

"Is it the best?"

"Ooh, yeeaaah."

"Is it the best?"

"Mmm, hmmmm. Mmm, hmmmm."

Janeia reached her left hand to the blond wig she wore in the hallway and began to cry. It hurt so damn bad. It was the kind of pain that stopped your heart from pumping, shot poison into your brains, made your gums hurt, your eyes burn, your nose run, and your fingernails rake your own skin.

And the worst part of the pain was that she would never feel Molasses's sweet stroke again . . . before she sent his ass to hell.

IN the twilight of morning, Molasses sat up in bed and could see a clear vision of Janeia Goode's eyes. They stared at him with all sincerity on Lake Michigan. And he found himself with no real reason to leave her. She could really be the one. He just had to figure out how to make himself commit to her.

He looked over at the clock on the nightstand—it read 5:27 AM. His hot date for the night was still sound asleep.

So Molasses took a breath and decided to take his shower. But before he went in, he grabbed his nickel-plated nine, which he had hidden inside his suit jacket.

He entered the extralarge bathroom and locked the door.

JANEIA must have walked past the door in the hallway at least forty times that night, just waiting for Molasses to take his shower. That was his MO. As dirty as his life was as a hired killer, he loved to be clean. So as soon as she heard the shower water running in the bathroom, she made her move on the door.

MOLASSES finished his shower, dried himself off, and walked back out into his hotel bedroom with only a towel wrapped around his waist. He hid his gun back inside the closet with his suit jacket and pants. There would be no more showing off his lifestyle to innocent women. He understood that now as his rule number six.

It was nearly six in the morning, and the early rays of the sun were beginning to peek through the blinds in the room. So his date had decided to cover her head under the sheets to block the light from her eyes.

Molasses smiled in her direction and approached the bed.

"Rise and shine time, girl. Don't you have work today? Where do I need to drive you?"

As he continued to talk to her through the sheets, he heard the familiar sound of a silencer pistol.

Theessrrpp!

He suddenly jerked backward and grabbed his right armpit. He had been shot, and blood was quickly running down his right side. He looked toward the bedsheets as if it was a dream. It only took another second before he moved toward his gun in the closet.

But, before he could reach the closet for his gun, Janeia Goode pulled back the bedsheet. She was holding her own silencer gun and wearing black leather gloves. She was fully clothed and bent on vengeance.

She told Molasses with bloodshot eyes, "Stay where you are."

She wasn't about to let him reach his gun.

Molasses ignored her and continued to move.

She then shot him through his left hand as he reached for the closet door.

Theessrrpp!

"*Shit!*" Molasses hollered.

He was shocked that she meant business, as if he didn't realize that after the first time she shot his ass.

He froze after the second wound and turned to face her.

"I thought you said you fuckin' loved me."

Fresh blood ran down his fingers and his right side as he cringed from his two gunshot wounds.

Janeia looked at him calm and collected, just like he would have done.

She said, "I do love you, Molasses. I just have some rules of my own now."

Even though she was killing him slowly, he cracked a smile.

He said, "Charlie was right. Women and business is *bad* business."

Janeia told him, "You should have thought about that yesterday."

Molasses thought again about reaching for his gun, but her eyes were locked on him. So he knew not to move.

He began to look around the room for signs of the other woman.

"You're thinking about your little friend?" Janeia asked him. She slowly shook her head.

"She didn't make it. You know how the saying goes, 'Wrong place, wrong time.' "

Molasses paused. He was still trying to figure out a way to negotiate himself out of his predicament without sounding like a sucker. And to tell her that he had been thinking about her, and about them being together exclusively, would have sounded like a sucker move at the present. It was a little too late for her to believe that shit.

"So . . . what kind of rules are you workin' wit'?" he asked her. He figured he'd humor her for a minute, to lighten things up.

Janeia was straight-faced when she answered him.

She said, "I told you that I loved you, right? So my rule number one is to make sure you love me back."

Molasses could read the coldness in her bloodshot eyes. She had stayed up and cried outside of his door all night long. So he raised his hands to surrender to her.

"Wait a minute. I . . ."

Theessrrpp!

Janeia shot him in the chest before he could finish his sentence. And as Molasses leaned in agony toward the closet again for his gun, she continued to shoot him.

Theessrrpp!
Theessrrpp!
Theessrrpp!

Before he fell to the foot of the bed, his eyes showed remorse. But he was a day too late with his phone call, and had one bitch too many in his bedroom.

Janeia climbed out of the bed and stepped over the dead woman on the floor by the wall.

She then walked over and stared at Molasses's body, still leaning up against the foot of the bed.

She said, "We could've had a good thing going, Molasses. But you just fucked that up. And now look at you."

She slipped the silencer gun and the leather gloves back inside of her large black purse, and took a final look at Molasses's dead body.

But there was no more love left in her eyes. Her usual warm stare had been replaced by a cold glare of righteous vengeance. She felt he had deserved it, not only for her but for all of the women he had played.

So she slid on her dark shades and blond wig and headed for the door.

Did I feel remorse after killing Molasses? Of course I did. But after a while you just gotta get over it.

Two months later in the Chicago cold, a public transportation bus pulled up to the Chicago State University campus. Several college-age students climbed down from the steps with their book bags and personal things, including Janeia Goode. She was dressed in warm clothes and a bright green scarf, nothing fancy.

Officer Barrett popped up on the campus grounds himself that morning. He was dressed in the plainclothes of a detective and reading an old newspaper article. It was about Warren Hamilton, the infamous Molasses, who had been shot to death, along with a female companion, inside a Maximum Hotel room downtown.

Officer Barrett spotted Janeia and approached her with a slight grin.

"Janeia Goode. How are you these days? Have you been bad recently?" he asked her.

She looked over the familiar cop's comfortable dark suit and electric blue tie and ignored his comment.

"I see we're moving up in the world . . . *Detective*," she said to him.

"Don't we all," he told her.

She paused and said, "Well, I don't mean to be rude, but if you'll excuse me, I have to get to class."

"You're studying psychology, huh?" he asked her.

Janeia nodded and kept walking.

"If you already know, then why do you ask?"

Officer Barrett spoke to her back, "That's a good question."

But Janeia never stopped to acknowledge his response.

When she was out of earshot range, he told himself, "I guess I still believe in innocent until proven guilty." He looked down at the newspaper article and added, "Even when I know you're guilty."

He folded the article back in his hand and walked off.

JANEIA took a seat in her new class for the winter semester just as the lady professor began her lecture.

"Just to start us off on an honest foot here, I hope we all understand that the field of clinical psychology can be grossly underappreciated in the American workforce. However, I believe I feel like most of you in this room when I say that everyone could benefit a great deal from more psychological expertise on the job, and in society in general. That way we can all understand a bit more why people choose or *don't* choose, for that matter, to do the things that they do."

Janeia sat back in her seat, pulled out her notepad and pen, and gave her instructor her complete attention. And while the lecture continued at the front of the class, she wondered if she could kill again . . . and get away with it.

About the Author

THE URBAN GRIOT is the pen name of Omar Tyree, the bestselling author of *Diary of a Groupie, Leslie, Just Say No!, For the Love of Money, Sweet St. Louis, A Do Right Man, Single Mom,* and *Flyy Girl.* As The Urban Griot, he has written *College Boy, The Underground,* and *One Crazy-A** Night.* For more information, view his website at www.theurbangriot. com. The soundtrack recording is available through Hot Lava Entertainment at www.hotlavaentertainment.com.